# S.

# THERAPY

# Sonny Vincent

www.farwestpress.com

First Edition

ISBN 978-1-7365388-0-7

Printed in the United States of America

This book is dedicated to Steve Conway. Special thanks to Francesca, Eva Ventura, Dee Dee Drunkwater, and Willie. Soulful thanks to all my friends who supported me when I had nowhere to turn.

# Introduction

I've always written short stories, poems, and songs. When I was a kid my cousins and I would skip school and we would immediately proceed downtown, grab a slice of pizza, a Coke, and then begin a day of discovery, vandalism and other exciting juvenile delinquent activities. That included everything from breaking into random buildings, churches, squeezing super glue (our new passion) into every lock we came across, throwing endless rocks at everything and, in general, expressing our distain for society, culture, and life itself. But more often than not I would skip school solo and go by myself into the woods. I spent the whole day in the woods writing stories, poems, laying on my back in the leaves sleeping and praying to the trees, birds, the squirrels, and the bits of sky that were peeking out between the leaves to save me. I never received a communication back from the animals, flora, and fauna but I still believed.

I knew when it was time to leave the dark woods because I was signaled by the sounds of cars driven by moms going to fetch their kids from school after their full day of social indoctrination and learning.

I went to an Ivy League College Prep school that was Junior High and High School together in a building that looked like a small Notre Dame. A very affluent town that provided a Norman Rockwell atmosphere for families comprised of old money, Dads who commuted to their corporate jobs in Manhattan and the other elite. A real Stepford community. I hated it and didn't fit in. Later in life I moved to the working-class area of the Bronx which I found to be more soulful. Anyway, here I was growing up next to hundreds of well-dressed clone kids looking like they were all related to Robert Redford. Redford, Stepford. I didn't fit. Rather than wear the de rigueur madras pants, Bass Weejun penny loafers, and corduroy slacks, I took my cue from movies that portrayed rebels. You might call it the "West Side

Story look." In my town the people who dressed like that were called "hoods." But being only 12 years old my image only confused the adults. My parents did not know, because every morning I would go to the woods where I had my clothes of personal choice hidden in a crevice in an old tree. There I would change clothes and experience a transformative shift in my self-worth. It felt good. The clothes were very cool. Pointy shoes, iridescent shirts, shirts with piping on the edges, and chequered or sharkskin slacks. The only other person in school who dressed like me was a Puerto Rican guy who had been left back a few times. He really looked more like an adult than a student. He walked through the halls very confidently giving out a vibe that was starkly different to the kids around me growing in their "Future of America" petri dishes.

Anyway, back to my story, writing in the woods and throughout my childhood.

I didn't really think of my writing much, it was simply part of me. Unfortunately, the home I grew up in was ignorant and most of my stories were usually found and then thrown away as if they were some communist diversionary propaganda. I would leave a good one on my dresser expecting a reaction, only to find it had been thrown in the trash. A lot of them that I wish I had today. But I did hide many in the woods and retained them. When I formed Testors some of the poems I had written at age 12 and 13 wound up as lyrics to songs I played at Max's Kansas City and C.B.G.B.'s.

Back to school days again. I really didn't fit in and really didn't care. Most of the teaching and voices during the classes sounded like strange chatter in an echo chamber to me. One time I did daydream about what a standard Junior High School English teacher would think of my poems and stories. But I didn't have the self-empowered confidence to submit them. I stayed in my loner bubble all through the tortures. Years later, after my forced enlistment into the United States Marine Corps, I was living in Portchester N.Y. raising a small family, working a job and playing in my band Fury. One day, my younger stepsister came to me with a problem. She was going to the same school, but much had changed since I was there. What was formerly a throwback to a kind of Victorian authoritarianism evolved into an egalitarian hippie, Beatles, '60s, new age education. Focusing obviously on liberal arts. The problem for my stepsister was that she had not been actively involved in her studies and she desperately needed to get a passing grade in her English class in order to graduate. Her teacher knew she was bright and although my sister Deb never turned in any work to be graded, he gave her an ultimatum. "Do one work. A book report, an essay, anything. I'll grade you for the year according to that."

Dang, maybe if I had cool teachers like that, I would have spent more time in school and less in the woods. Anyway, Deb came to me with her predicament. She didn't have a clue as to what she could come up with to submit. We sat there in my apartment talking about it and suddenly I went to my file cabinet grabbed a folder labeled "Sure Death." I took out 3 of what I thought were my best poems. I told Deb, "Submit these." Debbie submitted the three poems under her name as "writer" and her teacher said, "I'll read them tonight and get back to you tomorrow." The following day her teacher came in all flustered and proud that he had a little writer hidden amongst his class. He even made a verbal proclamation to the other students effusively introducing his discovery in Deb. He later submitted the poems to a periodical where Deb was lauded in print. Debbie had to recite *her* poems to the entire school body on graduation day and told me, "I even painted the poems on my bedroom wall, I'm so sorry, I got so much attention that something flipped in my head and I even thought I had written them." I said, "No worries Deb, I have tons of this stuff!

# First Job - Mrs. Rogers

Location: Rye, New York
Employer: Mrs. Rogers
Job Description: Yard work, housework, painting, carpentry, etc.

This was my first job. I was 12 years of age and I had read an advertisement in the local newspaper. It stated that a "Mrs. Rogers" needed a handyman to do various jobs around the house like painting, lawn work, and more. Although I realized that she was most definitely looking for a scruffy dude in his 30's to show up in a t-shirt and painting pants, I thought I might have a chance. Rye, New York was quite an affluent small town in Westchester and there was a major shortage of dudes in painting pants and t-shirts. There I stood 12 years old, a lopsided homemade haircut, skinny, buttoned-up shirt, and nervous as hell. I pushed the doorbell and Mrs. Rogers answered. She was about 65 years old, very polite, straightforward, and sweet-natured. I told her I was applying for the job advertised in the paper. She laughed a bit, not in a mocking way but in a pleasant kind of "laughing at life" way. She asked me if I knew how to paint and a few other things. I lied and said yes to her whole list. She invited me in. It was a grand Victorian-era mansion that Mrs. Rogers had transformed into a sort of English boarding house. Now that I look back it all seems very cinematic. Anyway, no sooner do I get inside then someone is coming down the well-carpeted stairs. He is introduced to me as Dr. Johnson, one of the tenants. He just grumbled something and shuffled off to another area of the house. The interior of the house reflected the accoutrements of wealth from many generations of the Rogers family. Everything in the place was a fine antique. We sat in the main living room as Mrs. Rogers explained to me that she needed help with small things around the house and garden. She spoke in a kind of wooden, "orator's" high voice. Direct, but not shrill. She outlined the many items that needed repair and went through a long list of chores. The place was beautiful, but it was falling apart. She then got a piece of paper and wrote a numbered list of the daily duties and elements of upkeep necessary in and around the big mansion. She always re-asked me periodically if I was an experienced painter. We spent hours together at that first meeting and during that time Mrs. Rogers gave me a detailed history of the house, its occupants, and herself. After many rounds of tea and cookies, I realized it was getting near dinner time and said I had to head home. We made an appointment for Saturday at 11:00 a.m. and my first job was to (of course) paint! I worked for Mrs. Rogers for about 8 months during the week and on weekends. My pay was 75 cents an hour, and all the tea, milk, cookies, and sandwiches I wanted. My most pleasant memory of this job is the vivacious manner of Mrs. Rogers and her way of making everyone feel special and respected.

# Playland-Second Job

Location: Rye, New York (at Playland)
Employer: Gannett Press
Job Description: Media Marketing

For many years, I had noticed that paperboys were always chewing gum. This was a tip-off to me that being a paperboy was most likely a lucrative position. In my town, paperboys would tear around on bikes and hurl rolled-up newspapers at houses. It was not only a seemingly lucrative job to have, but also had a built-in element of machismo. These factors, combined with the serious "I'm at work here so don't bother me" look all paperboys have as they roll up and prepare their newspaper grenades, convinced me that I should look further into the "News Game." I offered my assistance to the paperboy in my neighborhood. For a nominal fee and the occasional wad of gum. This was my way of finding out if being a paperboy was all it seemed to be. Well, it was and how! I learned the places that don't tip are the places that are designated for heavy artillery. The rolled up and rubber-banded newspapers can be used for all kinds of target practice, everything from flat out broadsiding a house to knocking over garden gnomes. I also learned that whenever a customer had a special agreement with the paperboy, such as delivery onto a porch or into a mail slot (which would require a dismount and a good bit of concentration, not to mention the disruption of target practice) there was always a gigantic tip associated with these requests for deviance. These tips represented a king's ransom to a kid. Although you could always detect an air of irritation on the face of the paperboy whenever he had to service these locations, due to the major inconvenience and the slight diversion in tactical maneuvers. At these houses, he meticulously carried out the big tipping customers' special requests. After I learned the route, the kid I worked for got the bright idea that I should try the route on my own (for training purposes of course). I did this and then subsequently I did the route by myself whenever he got sick. I soon learned that I was now doing his route all week for around a dollar per day (with no gum), while he merely showed up on Friday to collect the enormous amounts owed to him and the newspaper company for the week of delivery. This situation was soon to change. I had no interest in becoming this newspaper boy's sub-contractor, or worse yet a newspaper sharecropper.

I called the main office of the newspaper company and spoke to Ken Miller. We made an appointment to meet at my house the next day at 3:00 p.m. I didn't need much preparation for this meeting. Unlike other jobs, a newspaper boy position is more or less a wash 'n go situation. Just be somewhat presentable and be able to utter the word "collection" on Fridays and you're already in the top 95th percentile. Ken enters the living room. I expected an older guy, someone who had a visor or at least a tweed jacket. But no, what I got was a "Sparky" type. A college student working as a route manager, a combination of a supermarket bag boy par excellence and camp counselor. After the initial handshaking and sitting down, he tells me with a big Kennedy smile that there are no routes left in town and that there wasn't much of a chance that any would open up in the near future. There I sat dejected trying to maintain a semblance of hope, which was slightly bolstered by that smile of Ken's…somewhat. Although I was quite young, I had seen that smile before. It was the "ask not what your country can do for you" smile. In other words, my initial assessment of Ken/Sparky was right, he was a bag boy but one that was operating on a more sophisticated level. He was a politician and that smile on his face said to me that he wanted something from me, which he would now explain to me. It was in my own benefit and interest, but really it was a feather in his own cap. He said that although all the routes in town were taken, he had an idea of how he could open up a new route in a previously un-serviced location. Where? PLAYLAND! Playland is a small to mid-sized amusement park in this town. It has been there on the boardwalk on the Long Island Sound since the twenties. It's mostly made of wood and, regardless of new modern additions, maintains most of the original rides and attractions. It had a Kiddy Land (where all the rides are similar to the adult section only scaled down), a Fun House, Ye Olde Mill (an indoor boat ride mostly in the dark for lovers and those wishing to find a cool, calm, tranquil atmosphere within a scenic installation), The Dragon Coaster and all that you would expect from a complete amusement park, down to canoes that you could rent on the lake. Every Friday night Playland featured a huge fireworks display, lighting up the whole sky while reflecting a mirror image of the display on the water of the lake. Nice huh? Yeah, nice place to visit and have fun, but this guy wants me to hawk papers there!!!! I was crushed but mustered up as much enthusiasm as I could for Sparky. I'm sure he figured if I would take the bait and agree to open this new "route" he would be regarded as a golden boy by his bosses and colleagues back at the office for his ambitious and creative expansion in the face of harsh limitations. Yeah, one can only speculate what enterprise old Sparky is up to these days. So, I did it, I figured it was better than no route at all and even though I didn't believe Sparky when he promised me the first available "real" route, there was a glimmer of hope in my soul that someday I would be a normal real paper boy. My first day was predictably embarrassing. On the corner where all stacks of bound unrolled newspapers were dropped off by the company truck, there was a new stack with my name on it. The first encounter on this corner with the regular paperboys was a sort of pecking order adjustment. None of them ever realized that the day would come when a new route would be created thereby raising their status to a kind of

"Executive Paper Boy" level. I was to be this denominator.
I felt a bit lowly at this corner encounter and could feel
the jabs and snubbing sent my way by this new elite.
Rather than stay around and prolong this humility I
grabbed my stack (no need to roll them on my route)
and walked off bike-less (a common foot soldier) to
Playland. I arrived and wanted to first try my luck where
the highest concentration of activity was. I walked
directly to the center of the amusement park where all
crossroads met and began to yell "Paper!" "Paper!"
"Daily paper!!" This went on for an hour or so with no
one buying a paper from me. I really began to feel stupid.
I had only seen this sort of paper selling in old James
Cagney movies by guys wearing gloves with the fingers
cut off and funny hats on. If maybe I sold one, just one
paper in these first crucial moments I might even have
had the self-esteem to feel like I was one of these people
from the movies bellowing out, "Paper! Paper! Get yer
Paper." I could just play it off as sort of an acting role.
But I just felt low... lower than low. My kingdom for
some fingerless gloves and one sale. But no. No interest.
Only strange looks and a kind of "what the fuck?"
curiosity. I began to analyze my situation. I came to the
conclusion that there was a vital and major flaw in good
old Ken's bright idea. People coming to an amusement
park really don't have the time or the desire to curl up
with a fresh copy of the local newspaper and catch up
on current events and school lunch menus, especially
when the people at the park are in from areas all over
New York state and points further. I tried the beach, and
I tried the picnic area. At this time, I did sell a couple
(meaning two at 25 cents a pop), but I could sense these
were kindness or in my case mercy purchases. They were
friendly people who wanted to help a kid out and most
likely didn't even read the paper. I hope they at least used
it to soak up some spilled coke or to wrap a porcelain
curio they might have won at the dart game. All in all, I
was walking around like a dazed zombie only occasionally

getting up the courage to yell out "Paper!" Finally, when some cute girls started laughing at me, I knew something would have to change, and quick. I was headed for suicide or homicide. Or to be more descriptive, "Sparky-cide." I could just envision him sitting at his desk at the newspaper office, stretched out with his feet up on the desk, puffing on a cigar and dreaming that he was to become the next William Randolph Hearst. Meanwhile, here I was getting laughed at by girls my own age. Yes, something had to change. I turned and walked up a wooden ramp and then through an archway with a sign that read "Entrance." When I reached the top of the ramp, I met a guy sitting on a chair next to a wooden box, the box had an open slot for tickets to be deposited into. He was the operator of this ride called "The Whip." He seemed to be a nice fellow just sitting there waiting for customers, enjoying his slack summer job of collecting tickets, pushing a button twice, and then opening an exit gate. Yes, you do detect an air of jealousy here. I approached him and asked him if he would like to buy a paper. He smiled and began jostling me. Asking how it came to be that I was selling papers in this manner. I brushed off his puns by saying it was just a temporary thing until a normal route opened up. I then suggested that on pauses like this it might be nice for him to have something to read. He agreed that this was true but said he didn't really want to spend the money on it. Then he said something that was to open a new vista in all my future transactions concerning these (now quite heavy) newspapers and Playland. He said, "Well I don't want to buy one, but I'll trade you a ride for one o' them newspapers." I jumped at the opportunity to get rid of one of the papers and took him up on his offer. After an enjoyable ride I collected my stack of papers and without further ado approached the guy running the next ride, "The Caterpillar." I made him the same offer, a paper for a ride. In what seemed to be no time at all, I made my way through the entire amusement park trading my papers for rides and even traded some for games and food. By nighttime, all my papers were gone, and I was one tired but slaphappy paperboy. This went on for a couple of days until I was suddenly gripped by a terrifying fear. At the end of all this fun, I had no money. None for me, none for Sparky, none for the newspaper company, none, nada, zippo, zilch. During the exhilaration of this joyride, I had lost track of economics. For two days, I would pick up my stack of papers and run down to Playland for free rides, using my papers as tickets. I was not a slacker and didn't want to get stung at the end of all this, but I didn't know what to do to resolve the situation. Friends suggested I tell Sparky that my papers were stolen from the corner, but this wouldn't work to explain a week's worth of missing funds, and it was a coward's way out (with quite frankly too many holes). I may have been the best foot soldier, but I was definitely not a deserter, I had to figure something out. But what? The next day I decided to take my cousin and our friend Arthur with me to Playland to accompany me on my rounds. All the way there I racked my brain for a solution to my predicament, with no results, and the most unsettling factor was that here I was on my way to Playland destined to repeat the same pattern of the last two days. A ride for a paper. Much to my amazement, the operators let all three of us all go on the rides for just the one paper. This gave me a new idea and a possible solution to my predicament. Start a "Rides for Paper Club." I calculated how much I owed the company each week and then once I knew the bottom line, money owed, I added a high-profit margin for myself. All these costs were met by charging a daily membership fee to each member of the club. Normally, a ride for a kid was a dollar in tickets, I was getting rides for the exchange of a newspaper worth 25 cents, which means me and my friends could go on the rides for a few pennies each. I began to bring more and more kids with me (while keeping it to a reasonable limit). I found that since I now

18

knew the ride operators on a daily personal level they were more than happy to let me, along with any number of friends, have a free ride in exchange for a paper. By charging a nominal fee to these newfound business partners (kids from the neighborhood who each chipped in a small amount of money to go on rides etc.) I was able to cover my weekly bill with Sparky, make a high profit for myself, and provide us all with a whole summer of wild times at Playland. A nice postscript to the story is that the entourage of kids was constantly changing all summer and most anyone we met was welcome in for a small fee. Or in needy cases, a deferred payment, which was a mere fraction of the actual cost of the access we were now afforded to the rides and concessions at Playland. Me and my pals, we were there each day, all day, all summer, and those girls that were laughing at me, well ... I must admit the real pretty one became my girlfriend that summer!! We had a blast!!! Man, we truly had the ride of every kid's dreams.

Thanks "Sparky" wherever you are!

# Kill Nature
# Before It Kills You

Good idea! Here's another.

We should get rid of all the whales once and for all. They are simply too big and very egocentric much like the SUV, in that they take up so much space and use more energy than should be allotted for a unit. Getting rid of the whales will only be a start. A symbolic gesture to somehow save the sanity of mankind. I suggest we pluck the whales out of the ocean each summer and lift them up into the sky with big helicopters that have a sling attached. Before we lift them, we insert a small bomb into the anus of the whale. We do this procedure when the giant fires start up each year in California. A beautiful solution. The whale is placed in the sling and picked up by the helicopter, the helicopter flies to the site of giant fires in California and hovers above while the whale is just hangin' there. With perfect timing, the 'copter drops the whale in the direction of the fires and flies away (really fast. Whirrrr!). When the 'copter is clear of the whale, the bomb is detonated so that all the whale flesh lands on the fires and puts the fires out! And of course, all that crispy whale meat can feed the homeless and supply fancy Japanese restaurants. O.K. Two problems solved, those pesky big whales...gone... and those dang giant yearly fires...out! But like I said it was only a symbolic gesture and the best comes next. After getting rid of the whales, we will soon realize that it would be quite easy to just get rid of the entire ocean, in fact, a simple procedure will free us from all bodies of water. We just invent a huge suction device using my "reverse gravity theory" and suck all the oceans into space with giant suction tubes. Then space can deal with all that flotsam and jetsam nonsense. There! Easy! We got rid of the Sea, including everything down there. Presto.

No more guilt about destroying the oceans. In fact, the whole process will continue in that direction. Get Rid of Nature (GRN). The main idea is to free mankind of all guilt. One of the major guilt issues we have is that we are destroying nature slowly...so.... being the clever humans we are, we know that all this guilt and stress is not good for us. And since we can't figure a way around our present slow death method of destroying nature, we should just get rid of it swiftly and save our peace of mind. Imagine the joy and global bonding we will experience during huge tribal bonfires where we burn ALL the trees! After we completely destroy all the forests, and nature itself, (except the "dominant" humans of course!), the first child will be born, a glorious, golden child, born with NO GUILT. Standing tall and proud knowing that he is the firstborn of a truly dominant breed. His mind will expand because he will not have the nagging guilt feelings humans have harbored for so long. And right away he will figure out new fun things for us! We will coat the Earth with solid CONCRETE. Even though there is not much left in the way of natural resources. The brainiac First Born Golden Child Without Guilt (FBGCWG) will sort out all the particulars. Yes! Coat the earth with concrete so we can all drive Ferrari's in any direction we want. Don't ask questions because once we get rid of this irritating thing called "nature" and we are free of all this stress and endless guilt we can do anything!!! Kill Nature Before It Kills You.

# My Stomach Hurts

Oh! My darling I saw your reflection in the highly polished gleam of a New Luster bowling ball. Ever since that day I have wanted to get on my hands and knees and suck the very sidewalk you walk upon. You have come into my life and left me with the feeling that a certified public accountant feels when he sensuously peels an orange. Valencia Gardens!! The Panama Canal!! A piece of gum under the glorious restaurant table. Exalt me with your angelic countenance. Excite me with your majestic ability to play "Wipe Out" on your stomach. You are like the air. You are like the drywall and the fiberglass insulation! You, my love, are bigger than the entire database of Google. You make me feel alive. You make me feel like I have lost one of my shoes and that's that. To proudly face the entire Midland Avenue Elementary School student body with but a shoe on one foot and a proud screaming sock on the other. The beautiful feeling of a shower. To bathe after not bathing for an entire seven thousand lifetimes is the way I feel when you plunge your tongue in my ear. And me a simple man a man of wood and stone. A man of plastic and hydrochloric acid. A man of sardine fluid and red licorice whips. I love you. I love you more than Chris Rock cloned with Lady Gaga. I love you more than a banana cream pie cloned with the very angels themselves. More, my Love, than Vincent Van Gogh cloned with Ethel Merman. My love, you are greater than a Barbie doll's breasts. You are more powerful than the need to use the toilet. You are my reason for going to the dentist. You are my total and complete unabridged Webster's dictionary. I am a 1,000-gallon load of jet airplane fuel. You, my love, are a beatific pack of matches.

# It's Only Plastic

I walked up to the boss I said, "You know I really like Formica!!!" The boss said, "You are wise my son, please stay a while and try to forget all the pain." I ran and I ran. My life before was now completely forgotten. I longed for plastic anything. I hadn't realized the importance of plastics. So, I ran. I ran through a mirrored corridor. It seemed like years. I ran and I knew my running was important to humanity. Only thinking of plastics and how they feel. Only thinking of plastics and how they taste. I could see myself in the mirrors. Side to side, ceiling, and floor. Of course, I removed my clothes. I was no fool. Running, running. I could hear the voices of childhood friends calling my name in an echo chamber. I rejected Hitler. Of course. Always running. You who are reading this. You. I give you one guarantee. Only one. I tell you the truth. You can learn from me. You might as well. You know and I know that you are running too. I wish I could stop for some plastic though. Just to taste it or burn it to smell. I swear these words and I know you know it's true. We are only running but it all is so fuckin' strange. I know it's important but at the same time, I feel controlled. We could stop here and smash the mirrors. But wouldn't that be a sin? That's the easy way. But I believe we're past all of that experimentation. It's the not knowing that makes me paranoid. Naked running. I will not fatigue. I will not doubt. They call out from history. You and I are running. Look into my eyes, my friend. Do you see it? I have no doubts. It's time to be strong. If we run for a million years, we will only get stronger. Everything is simple. Everything clear. Run my friend. Do not stop. You know you will never reach the end. It's a job we have found ourselves doing. Do it well. I see you doubting. That is no fault. That is normal. And we will never get bored. Because our running is perfecting the crystal. The environment will change but we will always run. We have trained for this forever. We have slept far too well for too many years. Get ready. We will never die. It is not possible because we have found forever in the eyes. My plastic heaven. So pure.

# All Dressed Up To Go
# To The Moon

Sonny Vincent: "Hey Sterling, a lot of people out there, me included got their vision of how to dress and look cool from looking at photos of bands like the Velvet Underground, the Yardbirds, and the Stones, but here you are 3 weeks into a tour, and you're dressed like a pud in those blue jeans and trekking boots!"

Sterling Morrison: "Yeah, but this is how I dress these days, it's all I have."

Sonny: "Well we're in London and there's a cool section called Camden Town, let's cruise over there and buy you some clothes so you can look cool again!"

Sterling: "O.K. you're my stylist then, let's go!"

So along with his credit card, we went off to Camden Town and I had total permission to dress him up.

"No not those shoes, Sterl. These Beatle boots. Yeah, and these black straight-leg pants." And so on...

We returned to the soundcheck at the Powerhouse with an Ex-Velvet rather than a tugboat Captain. In this story, I also want to show the beautiful, sweet, and brilliant nature of Sterling.

Other notes: Morrissey of The Smiths comes to the show in London and visits Moe backstage with his entourage. Truth is Moe didn't know who he was. Our promoter planted a story in the Melody Maker that said Moe wanted to meet Morrissey but actually that wasn't true. Moe had never heard of The Smiths, and although me and John Sluggette were fans of The Smiths, Moe never heard them till I played a tape for her the next day in the tour van.

Another conversation that happened around this time is one I had with Moe. I was telling Moe that I thought Sterling was a very special guy and different and I asked her what it was like when they were kids. Moe told me a story from their childhood.

Moe: "Something most people don't know about Sterl is that he is one of the most gullible people you will ever meet. We did a joke on him when we were kids. My brother Jim and their friends told Sterling that starting from age 13 a guy's penis began to shrink half an inch per year till he was twenty or something like that. Well, apparently Sterling believed it and was measuring himself like a maniac for years. It was quite funny how gullible he was."

Sonny: "That's really funny, I didn't notice that about him."

Moe: "You should try him some time, real gullible."

Traveling in a van with four or five people can be very funny and at times quite exciting but it can be a very boring time as well. Lots of sleeping, reading, and listening to music through earplugs. Sometimes you are wide awake, full of energy and everyone else is sleeping, No one to talk to. No one to make jokes with. Nothing to do but feel the drag of endless highway slipping under the wheels. After a while, I noticed that Sterling was very easy to activate into a long monologue speech. We even sometimes called him "the Pontificator." Also, Sterling often insisted on driving the van. Although we had drivers, he liked to be the Captain and probably felt safer driving himself. I soon discovered that at times when we were all awake, I could get Sterling to entertain us with his seemingly endless knowledge of life, earth, culture, people, and politics, to name a few of his areas of expertness. After all, he was Sterling Holmes

Morrison Ph.D. Anyway, sometimes on the long drives where we were all awake and bored to tears, I would suddenly come up with a spontaneous question for our in-house Ph.D.

Sonny: "Hey, Sterling what is the psychological disorder called when a person is wearing two kinds of shoes, you know like all the time going around with like a Moon boot on one foot and a sandal on the other? And the next day a sneaker on one foot and a Doc Marten boot on the other. Is there a term for that? Is it a disorder, a condition, or what?"

A question like that would invariably inspire Sterling to talk for hours, describing what he thought as the basis and content of the subject. In his speech he would bring us all through the subject citing everything from Freud to Marx, colorfully traveling in his dialogue to the cradle of mankind to a city street corner, Adam and Eve to the current political administration of the United States. And all during this we would just sit back in our seats and listen and be entertained by one of the most interesting people ever born. Of course, Sterling never knew he was being used for our entertainment on these long drives. I think he just enjoyed being the professor and we enjoyed it too. Anyway, this question about the two different shoes was about to evolve into one of the most insane particular pranks we ever played on Sterling.

We now call it The Moon Ticket Incident.

A little bit of set up here before I continue with the story. The seating arrangement was our usual, I was in the back seat on the far left, John Sluggette was to my far right near the sliding door. Moe was seated in front of me, also to the left; the bass player was on her right. Sterling was driving and the "driver" was in the passenger seat to his right. Suddenly, Sterling interrupted his flow and said, "Hey Sonny who was that with the different shoe thing?" Since there actually wasn't anyone and it was totally fabricated, I said, "Oh John's ex-wife, the one you saw in Paris." Now this statement of mine leads back to a prank that occurred a few days prior to this moment in the van.

We were playing in Paris and before the soundcheck, during the day, I hung around with Sterling hitting various shops and getting in the sights, but Moe and John Sluggette went to the record label offices for a visit. Apparently, Moe wanted to say "Hi" to the people who were handling her latest release. Later, Sterling and I met up with our bass-man Danny ("Good Danny") at the dressing room of the club we were playing that night and got prepared for the soundcheck. Right then Moe, John, and Patrick from New Rose Records and a very attractive woman entered the dressing room. I suppose since we were late for the soundcheck Patrick and the beautiful woman quickly kissed Moe and John Sluggette on the cheeks and exited waving to the rest of us. At that point, Sterling looked at me and said, "Whoa who was that girl? And why was she kissing John?" Well just to be a little idiot and mess with Sterling's head I said, "Oh that's his ex-wife but don't talk to John about it, it's a real sore spot for him." Most people who would look at John and then look at that woman probably wouldn't imagine that they were at one time together, but not Sterling he bought the story. Hook, line, and sinker.

Sterling: "Damn I didn't know John had it in him, she's incredibly beautiful."

Sonny: "Yeah, but just leave it, he doesn't like to talk about it, he only told me about it when he was drunk one time."

Sterl: "Man, I would like her number."

That's where we left it, just another little prank from me and just amusing myself. We then went to soundcheck and the subject never came up again until this ride in the van I was talking about. So back to the van.

Sterl: "You mean the one in the dressing room? She was the one who wears two different shoes?"

Sonny: "Yeah, you didn't notice it?"

Sterling drove on and I had to whisper to John the little prank I played on Sterling in Paris I explained that I said to Sterling it was a sensitive issue. But I wasn't done with this and began building on the story.

Sonny: "John, didn't you tell me when you were way drunk that her Dad was super rich and in the French Parliament? And didn't you also tell me that your love letters to her are in frames and displayed in the Louvre?"

Of course, John kicked right in with the timing of a seasoned comedic straight man. Spoken sadly.

John: "Yes, but I don't wanna talk about it."

Sonny: 'But that time when you were drunk you told me a lot. That must have been weird for you, like you told me, on your honeymoon night. Was she really playing Pacman wearing a moon boot and sandal?"

John: "It was real sad."

Sonny: "Is it right, do I remember it right that she had a Pacman machine delivered to the Hotel room and on the nuptial night you didn't even make love? She just stood there in the Moon boot and sandal playing Pacman?"

John: "Yes Sonny, but I don't want to talk too much about it, I always wondered what her problem was."

Sonny: "Hey Sterl what about that? Playing the Pacman machine in the two different shoes, how would a psychiatrist label that behavior?"

Then Sterling spoke for a while with some insights and opinions and I interrupted.

Sonny: "John, didn't you say her parents didn't like you very much?"

John: "Yeah, I wrecked a few sports cars down in Monte Carlo and lost around a hundred grand in the casinos one weekend."

Sterling: "Dang a hundred grand."

Sonny: "So John, back then you were really thin and had that pencil mustache with the full-length white tuxedo?"

John: "Oh yeah, we were on the cover of Boulevard Magazine."

Sonny: "Man, John you were on a roll. A super-rich beautiful wife, tons of money, and the toast of Paris. Do you still have some of those magazine articles?"

John: "Nah, but I do have that cover. I'm in the white Tux and she is in a beautiful evening gown, and we're holding champagne."

Sterling: "Damn, John I never picture you like that. Her parents didn't like you though?'

John: "No, they were really dogging me. They said I was a bad influence and spending too much money."

Sonny: "You were a bad influence? Didn't you say that her boyfriend before you was Jim Morrison?"

John: "Yeah but I was pretty wild at the time."

Sterling: "Damn John, the toast of Paris."

Sonny: "I guess they had lots of famous guests at the Villa, who did you meet?"

John: "Well, actually Bob Hope came by and all kinds of people. The strangest stuff happened when the Pope visited from the Vatican."

Sonny: "Like what happened?"

John: "We were having dinner and I had a little too much wine, but it seemed like the Pope liked me, he was sitting right next to me at the dinner table and we were talking about his younger years in Poland. He told me when he was a kid, he was a big boxing fan and he said he really liked the boxer, Rocky Marciano. Anyway, like I said I had too much wine, but everything was going great. I said to the Pope that I also liked Rocky Marciano and I got kind of excited and I started play boxing in the air as I spoke, jabbing and ducking and then suddenly I was jabbing toward the Pope and accidentally nailed him on the chin with a pretty hard punch and he fell backward, over the chair and landed knocked out on the floor. It was horrible, people were all running around in total shock and hysteria with smelling salts and everything."

Right then Sterling blurted, "Damn John you decked the Pope?"

At this point, we had to get gas and, of course, Captain Sterl was pumping the gas into the van himself so as none of us whippersnappers could screw up the tanking procedure. Me and Moe were buying water and stuff in the little shop inside the gas station and I asked her, "Moe this is incredible, is there a point where Sterling is gonna say 'Come on now this is bullshit!'"

Moe: "I don't think so."

Sonny: "But there has to be a point where he says that I'm really stretching the story beyond belief."

Moe: "Try telling him you went to the moon."

Sonny: "You think he will know then that it's all made up?"

Moe: "I don't think so, just try it."

We climb back into the van and on the road again.

Sonny: "John, I know that you are sensitive about it but was it true what you told me, that your ex-wife still is in love with you and she sends expensive gifts to you all the time?"

John: "Yes, but Linda doesn't like it."

Suddenly, Moe decides to join in, "Oh, I don't like that shit, she should leave you two alone."

John: "Yeah, I don't even open the boxes anymore, we either throw them out or stack em' in a closet."

Sonny: "But what about you John, you said you still have feelings?"

John: "It's really, really hard, she broke up with me and now I can't be around her or be too close because it's all so painful and I break down."

Sonny: "But what are you gonna do with that Moon Ticket you told me about?"

Danny: "Moon ticket? What's that?"

Sonny: "Correct me if I'm wrong John, apparently, there is a guy in Texas who is privately financing and building a real spaceship that will go to the moon, and part of the way he finances it is by selling tickets in advance. When you and Marie first got married one of your wedding presents was a "Moon Ticket" for each of you, right?"

Reader: You gotta be with me here and get the whole impact of this all. I am saying "Moon Ticket" over and over to make it sound utterly preposterous. Anyway...

Sonny: "John who else is going to be on that flight?"

John: "Oh, Liz Taylor and Michael Jackson are sitting

near each other, also I heard Madonna bought a ticket, all kind of stars and rich people."

Sonny: "But you said your ticket and your ex-wife's seating are right next to each other and you don't want to go."

John: "No, I don't want to go at all, it doesn't matter where I would sit, I couldn't bear to go, so I'm not."

Sonny: "Hmm, where is that Moon Ticket?"

John: "It's sitting there in my dresser in the drawer with my socks."

Sonny: "Didn't you say there was a place on the back where you could just fill in someone else's name and transfer the Moon Ticket over to someone else, so they could go to the moon instead of you?"

John: "Yeah, it's totally transferable."

Sonny: "And you don't want it, and after you sign it the other person owns it and goes to the moon next to your ex-wife instead of you."

John: "Yup."

Now there was dead silence in the van. The story was improvised and now fully told.

After about one-minute Sterling began clearing his throat, coughing, and he says loudly, "Um John, I'd be interested in that Moon Ticket if you don't want it."

John: "No problem Sterl. When the tour is over, I'll sign it over to you."

Sterling: "Thanks man."

Now it is silent again except for the muffled squeals we were making as we all looked into each other's eyes in utter amazement. Sterling really believed the whole story: John the "Boulevardier." Knocking out the Pope. Race car driver. And now Sterling is going to the moon!!!

# My Evil Little Krishna

**Page 1**

Sea of nails

    see me fail.

        But it's just got to be

        my own form

        of history.

The justice scales,

    and gutted whales,

        but it's just got to be

        me

            in

                eternal

                    ec –

                        cen –

                            tri –

                            city.

Neo-nazi, Paparazzi, Jew Ju jit su, da da trotsky, Hotsy totsy, tipsy turvey, a special kind of way that's a little nervy. Worship Seth after death. Keep a lid on when you microwave.

> And then the truth hurt
>
> but then the truth was just a lie.
>
> And the president called me
>
> on the phone

for permission to kill the Pope and shoot dope. Dope with hope. The hangman's rope. Such a narrow vision in the telescope. I shot dope with the Pope. But then the pope couldn't cope. And there wasn't any soap. The pope said yeah, and I said nope. I said nope to the Pope. And nope to the rope. Then the dope shot the dope. The president shot the Pope. Dope shot pope. Pope shot dope. Promenade your partner who hangs from a rope. I lost the left side of my brain. I saw a hundred thousand virgins in the rain. I lent all my money to the driver of the train. All the Catholics involved had to move to Spain. The rain in Spain falls mainly in my pain. In my pain I am insane. My name is pain ask me again I'll tell you the rain. Just like Able and Cain. Just like Clark Gable and Citizen Kane. Down, down, down, down the drain. Look and see the telltale stain. Don't talk to me when I'm in my astral plane. She's so plain. In the main she was plain. But I didn't complain. It was only a slight case of ball and chain. Mr. Ball and Mr. Chain went down the drain. Took a look around but it was all in vain. I worship on my knees the sovereign state of Main. The rain in Maine is better than in Spain. I'm talkin' plain. Like an oncoming train. Words can rhyme. The feeling went away in time. Just when her pussy was prime. You got yours and I got mine. And we're both just living on borrowed time. I admit to the crime. The crime is mine. And they all danced like devils at the thirteenth chime so ugly despised and negative. Negative human negative. Hopeful blissful negative. Yeah, I got my cravings, but I spent my savings, cravings, savings, ravings. Death, death, death, rhymes. Meth, meth, meth, methedrine that German chatterbox won't shut his mouth.

## Page 3

Page 3 is happy, oh Lord happy is the page that is 3. The page that is 3 is happy oh Lord.

Wait! No! Page 3 is just a lie. Page 3 doesn't even try. Page 3 you let me down and I cry. Page 3 broke my heart now I feel like I could die. I'm hurt real bad and I wonder why. Page 3 is just a lie. Page 3 took a knife and stabbed me in the back. Track, tac, pack, knack, crack, sack, hack. Hack and pack Hackensac. Snackpac.oh no! What now? Page 3 is dead. Get that through your head. Page 3 and Satan were wed. During the operation page 3 bled. So, they chopped off page 3's head. At least that's what they said. In matters concerning dread. It all went to page 3's head. And even though page 3 was good in bed. They made page 3 swallow liquid lead. Page 3 and the devil bred. They had sex in bed then off with the head. The devil and page 3 bred. Now the ego must be fed. Blood red. Ego must be fed. The devil and page 3 bred. And now it is said that in that bed page 3 bled. And bred. Page 3 and the devil opened the door. Page 3 and the devil gave birth to a whore. They fucked and fucked till the devil was sore, right in the middle of the spiritual war. It was all too important to just ignore. We had to know it all, we wanted more. The devil and page 3 opened a door. They fucked in the bed and gave birth to a whore: PAGE 4.

## Page 4

Now page 4 became a ruler of the underworld. All snakes and all tombs and all in the cherry flavored way. Between you and me and under the cuff. Page four is a sissy that's been acting tough. Page 4 is unattractive and not worth a dime. Not even a rhyme. Picture-car, television-god, responsibility-daydream, Auschwitz, serenity-ignorance, ignorance-telephone, dead frog carcass-caramba, education-not a chance, girlfriend-typewriter. Very nice, kama-sutra - Bo Diddly, breasts-fruit, pussy-now, psychodrama, Rorschach test - incredible - exciting, base instinct – revolving tenement house-stairs, stairway to heaven, foppish English groups - that's correct. The scary connection between Hitler and the Beatles - lock this guy up! It's only your mother, fever-pitched – James Brown, Las Vegas - whore, white-dressed nuns - beauty, the desires of Joe Average – predictable, primitive – naked, perfume pussy, pussy - manna, saying swear words too much - trying to be honest, guide children, horror - parent, desert island – records, prison - scumbag home, home - sigh, death – joke, joke – Muhammad Ali – nice guy, Benito Mussolini – fat, Hitler – retard, Australia – balls, good ole grandma – disappointing military school – razor burn, opinion or page 4 – wimpy but honest.

## Page 5

Page 5 is the eternal do-gooder. Page 5 is aware of the tribulations of page 1,2, 3, and 4. Page 5 is a liberal. Page 5 wants you to know that it is tolerant of pages 3 and 4. Tolerant isn't the right word though. Page 5 wants to send the message that "Sure I'm aware of the darker side of life." Page 5 even read Aldous Huxley and Genet but damn it, Page 5 wants to look at the brighter side of life. Sure, sure of course Page 3 and 4 are correct. Page 5 agrees that life is basically a piece of shit but darn it! Page 5 just wants to bring some sunshine into things! Come on get up off your ass. It's springtime and Page 5 wants to embrace life with a gosh dam positive attitude. Oh, I can see that sneer. Don't act so fuckin' intellectual. Page 5 is not a parody. Page 5 means it! Let's look at the bright side! Come on, you got it! In fact, page 5 would like to share a little secret with you right now! Page 5 and Page 6 have kind of decided that there should be more optimism around here. So, they painted up the neighborhood in fresh white paint and happy carnival colors. So, get ready cause - ta-da Page 5 and Page 6 say surprise it's a surprise party for you!! Hi!!! Look at all these smiling faces. Page 5 and Page 6 think you are the most wonderful person ever. And we are just happy to be here with you! Page 5 and Page 6 have arranged a very special present for you. Go ahead and turn the page!

PAGE 5 AND PAGE 6 present images for you. Get ready! We love you! Here it is! Just because you're you! Oh, you're soo cute! Ok. 1, 2, 3, close your eyes! 4, 5, 6, no peeking! Ok, 7, 8, 9, 10! Puppies, flowers, sweet cute bears, babies splashing in the tub, chocolate champagne, television, springtime, Paris, a cuddly night beside the fireplace, embracing, a tear of joy from the corner of the eye, honeysuckle, softness, gentleness, balloons, clowns, ferris wheels, popcorn, a ride in the country, a nice gift for you, breakfast in bed, bicycle ride to the lake, swimming, dogs, splashing, sun, warm, free, happy, jumping, squirting water, totally wet, kissing, lick, candy, juice, heart-shaped candy, vacation, sun, holiday, friends, friendly people, you are loved, you are welcome, you're so nice, you are very smart, you are very sweet, you are my everything, you smell good, party, ride, you're going to get a hug right now! you're so considerate, your mother should be very proud of you, you are a joy to be around, fresh, alive, sweet, kind, beautiful eyes, you are driving me completely crazy with Love, I feel like I've known you all my life, sexy, hurray! jumping frogs, lily pads, laughing, running, rolling down a hill, boating, barbecue, friends, close friends, you're the one, life, carbon copy, vacuous hollow soul, definite distrust, scumbag, hack you to death, not worth living, lonely, lies, hatred, blackness. Wait, wait, help this is Page 6, don't leave the party. That's only Page 1. He is drunk. It's o.k. He's gone home now. Why are you leaving?

**Obituary**

Page 7 died last night at midnight in his home while writing his chapter of "My Evil Little Krishna." Page 7 committed suicide after briefly attending a party held by neighbors. The world knew Page 7 by the name "Countrified Bill." And his first book "Fucked Around" Page 7 was for many the voice of his generation. In recent years was working on a new book titled "Blinded by Darkness." Simon and Schuster his publishers have no comment about the book and deny any knowledge of the whereabouts of the nearly completed work. Page 7 will be sadly missed by a generation of people who kept his paperbacks in the back pockets of their jeans. As well as his series of books for children, he is survived by his parents and his sister. Funeral services will be held at the Fein Mortuary 1304 Bruckner Blvd., Bronx NY.

# My Adam's Apple Is In The Wrong Place

*Memories of Bob Stinson*

Bobby Stinson, the only band member I ever went to a psychotherapy session with. There is a lot to tell and I want to make it clear that the words you are about to read are the truth, the whole truth, and nothing but the truth! This is dedicated to the memory of Bob Stinson, my friend of many years, who just happened to be one of the greatest guitar players of all time. For those who don't know, I am happy to introduce this. Bob was the lead guitarist from the group the Replacements and after they booted him out, he joined my band. Along with being a genius guitarist, Bob was also one of the strangest, sweetest, and nuttiest characters I have ever met. I could write a whole book about him, really! Here are a few notable elements of an intense, highly charged, and funny story.

First off, some background, I moved from New York City to Minnesota where I eventually met Bob. After my NYC group Testors had broken up. The reasons I left NYC are discussed later in this book!

The year was around 1980...man! You will never know what it was like for me back then to move from the downtown area of New York City to Minneapolis, Minnesota. It was a real shock. Beautiful but different. These people were inviting me to go ice fishing for God's sake. AND I was wearing Beatle Boots! In shopping malls, kids pointed at me and said "Devo!" I guess that's the only "punk" thing they knew back then, at the time, because I think Devo was one of the first to get any airplay there and they had a video out. But a wonderful part about moving there was that the people were incredibly friendly. Quite open and different from the snotty NY attitude. After I got used to the slow driving and slow-talking natives, being there became a little bit easier on me.

When I arrived, I went to the cooler small clubs right away to see what was happening on the local scene. The first band I saw was Hüsker Dü and I was very impressed. Hüsker Dü right away reminded me of my former band Testors. I saw it all as a kind of brotherhood or shared vision. Groups and artists who obviously were more interested in being "real" than in commercial concessions. I was happy to see this was happening in Minnesota. Later I became friends with the guys in Husker Du, and eventually, the bass player (Greg Norton) was touring in my band for a while. To me, it was amazing that they even knew of the bands in New York because everything was so underground then, style and news traveled slowly. The media did not have this global machine like we have these days. Anyway, I was very very pleased and excited to see bands in Minnesota that had a similar spirit and energy. It was great because that's exactly where my head was at. I wound up staying there in Minneapolis with my girlfriend and I eventually found guys to form a band with. We called it Sonny Vincent and The Extreme (Mike Phillips, Mort Baumann, Jeff Rogers). We did tours of the U.S and recorded some songs in recording studios (songs that only much later saw the light of day). Every few months we would play a show in Minnesota either in Minneapolis or St. Paul. At one of these shows, it was at a club called the Upper Deck, I met Bob Stinson.

It was a double bill with my band and The Replacements. After the show, Bob came up to me and said, "I want to join your band." He said he would leave his band and that he and I could make a band together. Bob seemed sincere but I had to consider a few things. Bob was in a band that had done a lot of work, they had a very cool album out and just that week they had a fantastic review in my favorite New York newspaper, the Village Voice. I figured Bob was probably pretty drunk and I told him, "Hey Bob at this point I'm pretty much screwing around business-wise and to me, it looks like something is ready to break and go well for you guys, why the hell would you want to quit now?" Bob said, "Because I want to play your music." Well of course I didn't go for it and I didn't encourage Bob to quit his band. I thought the Replacements were a fantastic band, and they deserved everything they were working for. Of course, I didn't take Bobby's offer and just said, "You're nuts!" That was the start of our long friendship...

Later the Replacements kicked Bob out of the band. At that point, Bob and I started talking seriously about putting something together. Bob was in various band "formations" with me (as well as playing and jamming with other outfits such as Static Taxi and The Bleeding Hearts). In all the formations we put together the dynamic between our playing was usually the same. I was the singer and also played guitar, and Bob was the lead guitarist. I would play the basic root chords while Bob would play most of the leads and fills as well as cranking on the chords. His playing was amazing, often genius. But there is a whole story to his playing. To say it in a short form - when he was on- it was unbelievable. Stuff you never heard before. But when he was off, he would often not even hit the notes in the right key! This being said, I have to make it clear again that Bob was a guitar genius and a major shredder. Although sometimes inconsistent he played in a way that was magical and transcendental. Big words, but all true. The main thing was his feeling and realness within the song. He also played with a ferocious amount of concentrated energy, that more often than not would send a song right over the top.

Another thing that set him apart was his natural kind of symphonic approach when structuring his parts. This set him apart from most players, but it came with a heavy dose of chaos and unpredictability. That probably alienated people who wanted a more classic, conservative approach in their guitar heroes. Playing with Bob was a kind of schizo experience because sometimes it would really be great and other times it could be pretty awful. A lot of this had to do with alcohol and some of it was just classic "Bobby." This was his legacy of "Savant-ness" as we called it, and this behavior, of course, existed when he was in The Replacements too. Bob told me one story about them playing New Orleans and on this occasion, he somehow separated from the group and went to a bar. He got very drunk and then was lost. He didn't know the name or address of the venue and had to call his girlfriend all the way in Minnesota and said, "Baby, I'm separated from the band and I don't know where the club is." She looks at her copy of the tour schedule and said, "Bob, get a taxi right NOW! You are VERY late for the show. Get in a taxi and go to number 125 Bourbon Street!!" So, Bob does that. He gets in a taxi and the taxi drives him two blocks (a couple of hundred meters at the most) and Bob gets out, walks into the club where the band is already playing. The audience sees Bob and goes completely crazy, clapping their hands and cheering. He gets up on stage and the audience is ecstatic as Bob plays his incredible killer guitar magic. But people were unaware that the band hated him for this kind of shit. Anyway, this is the baggage I inherited, and we formed a band. My adventure with Bob was about to begin. It was challenging to say the least.

We formed the group Model Prisoners that went through two lineups. The first thing I noticed was that when Bob was way drunk, he often played guitar like he was a beginner, so I convinced him not to, and even forbid him from drinking before a show. Bob was kind of looking up to me as a sort of big brother figure and he liked it when I laid out rules for him. The problem with Bob not drinking was that when he was completely sober and straight, he played even worse! I soon found out that Bob was one of these special types of geniuses that could unlock his immense talent only when he had the right amount of alcohol lubrication. With the right number of drinks under his belt, he was doing brilliant stuff on the guitar that was never heard before. Like as if he was wandering around in the cosmos and bumping into new planets. The second formation of Model Prisoners was myself, Eric, and Jeff Rogers (Jeff had also been in Sonny Vincent and The Extreme with me). Eric was a kid from Minnesota who was totally thrilled to be playing in the band. He was a huge Replacements fan and even carved up his desk in high school with a knife writing "the Replacements." You can imagine he was on cloud nine when we asked him to play bass. But soon he was becoming very disillusioned. As I said, Bob was brilliant and brought a special element to my music, but at the same time he was also showing up drunk to rehearsals. We usually had to drive to his place and wake him up to get him to the rehearsal room. The routine would go like this: I would drive and pick up Eric first, then Jeff, and then we would drive to Bob's place. Then we would send Eric up to Bob's apartment. Bob was usually sleeping off a hangover or watching TV. At first, he would tell Eric to fuck off. He knew if he didn't come downstairs Eric would have to get me and I would go up there and motivate Bob by either giving him cold coffee or doing something that would irritate him so much that he would figure it's easier to get up than be tortured. So rather than let Eric get me, Bob would yell at Eric for a few minutes, even sometimes punch him, but he would finally come downstairs. This was always the best scenario because when Bob showed up on his own, he was usually pretty tanked.

We played a number of shows together, mostly in the Midwest areas like Minnesota, Wisconsin, and places like Chicago. Normally after a show, Bob would stay for hours in the girls' bathroom. At first, I would say, "Hey, where's Bob?" Then I would see him later and say, "Hey man, where were you all night?" He would reply, "In the girls' bathroom, that's where they all go." That was one of Bob's 'cracked' methods of meeting women. Unusual for mankind. But perfect for Bob. Hanging around in the girl's room saying whacky things! And if he met a girl in the main social area of the club, more often than not he would say as the first sentence of introduction, "Could you lift up your shirt?" Although this never really got much response from women other than disbelief or disgust. Sometimes Bob would hit the jackpot and I would observe him from across the room with a wild girl in front of him lifting up her shirt and showing him her tits. Amazing! Something I want to make clear at this point is that I am telling you stories about my friend Bob and being forthright and accurate to give you a little glimpse of this man. But in no way am I trying to put him in a bad light or trying to make him seem unattractive to his fans or people reading this. I loved Bob dearly in my heart and I miss him so very much. To be honest, you have to know that he was like so many other damaged people in this world...but for all his mistakes and screw-ups I can tell you he had a golden soul and a quality of innocence that you rarely find.

Anyway, that being said... Bob also had many juvenile tricks. In the beginning, directly after shows, he would go to the promoters of the show and collect the money, "Yeah, Sonny told me to get the cash" ...before any of us knew what he was doing, he would run off with our gig money and we wouldn't be able to find him for a week! Soon everyone wanted to kick Bob out of the band (not me but mostly Eric!). I finally had to call Bob and tell him the sad news that the other guys wanted to kick him out. Bob started crying on the telephone saying that we can't kick him out. He said he loved playing the music and he was sorry for everything... "But please don't kick me out." I got off the phone and decided I would be a fool to kick out a brother who was crying tears because he loved music so much. I called everyone in the band, and I made a plan for us to go to a therapist together to try to get Bob more healthy and easier to work with.

People thought that was pretty funny. A band going to therapy together. But we tried it. It kept us together for a while but still, the crazy shit didn't stop. In fact, it got worse. One night after a show in Milwaukee we all took some L.S.D called Rambo. Of course, suddenly Bob was missing, and we had to drive around for 3 hours to find him. Finally, we did and started our journey back to Minnesota. It was the most bizarre drive you can imagine. Bob was grabbing his throat the whole time screaming, "My Adam's Apple is in the wrong place, but my mom will fix that with the devil!"

While we were driving through the vast farmland areas of Wisconsin, we began to calm down a bit. Bob said, "Sonny if you can write a song that farmers will listen to while milking cows, it will be a big hit." We started getting crazy again and came up with a lot of perfect cow milking songs as well as all singing every Elvis Presley song for hours. Completely nuts and over the top. We arrived home in Minneapolis at Lyle's bar just in time to drink all day. The whole band was BECOMING Bob.

Eventually, we simply stopped rehearsing as it was becoming more and more difficult to get Bob out of bed and Eric had become a shattered person. Instead of practicing, me and Eric just started hanging around as pals for a few months going out to clubs and stuff. Then I put together a new lineup called Shotgun Rationale, as well as joining Moe Tucker's band as her guitarist. My band Shotgun Rationale was doing a lot of tours in the U.S., Canada, and Europe. At that point, I had given up on the band concept. We had a rotating line-up (Bob, Cheetah, Greg Norton, Mort, and many others). I liked it this way because I could invite people into it without any long-term expectations. Later I moved to Europe but still recruited various musicians from New York and Minnesota to join me on Euro tours with Shotgun Rationale. At the time I also did U.S. tours and sometimes visited Minnesota from time to time. Whenever I went to Minnesota, I would contact Bob and we would hang out together. He always said, "Hey Sonny you bring all these guys with you to tour Europe, but you never ask me! Come on I wanna tour with ya'l!"

Finally, I invited Bob. We did a tour of Europe together somewhere in the mid-'90s and sure enough, it was totally insane. To Bob's credit he really practiced the music hard before the tour, he wanted it to be great. And it was. But it came complete with every sort of crazy madness imaginable!

There are so many examples and I can only name a few here. Everything from Bob copping drugs from an audience member while on stage during our show, to him going into a whorehouse to drink because he would be out of our reach and control in there. Police, puking, broken guitars, blood, nakedness, tears, and insane shows. I often get together with friends from those times and I even have to double-check with them to see if I am imagining some of the preposterous things.

A mutual friend of mine and Bob's was Jamie Garner. Jamie actually at one time lived in the same apartment with Bob. Years later, I found myself asking Jamie questions like, "Hey Jamie do you remember Bob always ate his meals with two chairs, one chair to sit on and one to put his plate on?" Jamie said, "Yeah, he did that all the time." You see I often have to recheck these memories because sometimes they seem too bizarre. Bobby never ate his meals at a table, it was ALWAYS two chairs. Bob also had the ability to pull many beers out of his pockets at the best moments. In fact, the first day I went out drinking with Bob he even pulled a fried chicken leg out of his pocket and ate it. That's not so strange but in Bob's case, there was always a twist. He pulled an UNWRAPPED fried chicken leg out of his trouser pocket. It was just in there next to his keys and stuff... I guess he was saving it for the perfect moment. There he sat at the bar with me, chomping on that chicken leg. It had pocket fuzz and old tissue on it! Bob was a strange motherfucker and I guess to an extent so am I, so we got along fine. He was a rare person and I miss him. Sometimes I'm doing something fun and I often think of him and wish he could be there with me. We did many things together, we had side jobs painting houses, we were constantly being pulled over for speeding in my '59 Cadillac and we were always in trouble with the police. But throughout all of this, Bob would crack very funny dry jokes.

When Bob first started playing with me, he didn't have a guitar. After the Replacements told him he was out, he sold his guitar, and he got a job washing dishes at a diner on Lake Street. Eventually, Tommy, his brother, lent him a vintage Gibson SG but after a month or so Tommy needed it back. So, for the remainder of our playing together, Bob used my second guitar which was a vintage 1970 Les Paul Black Beauty. I played a 1969 Black Beauty Fretless Wonder. Bob used Dean Markley Strings. I used Ernie Ball. For amps, we both had Marshalls. 100 WATTS. One time back then I called an old pal, Cheetah Chrome, in New York. I told him about the band I had with Stinson in Minnesota and invited Cheetah to come out and join. I knew it would be a short-lived line-up because both of those guys were on a kind of short fuse at the time, but I also knew it would be a real unique once in a lifetime event getting those two playing in the same band for a while.

Cheetah came out to Minnesota from NYC. He brought a strange white guitar. I don't remember but I think it was maybe a modified Strat. I could also write a book about Cheetah in Minneapolis, what a crazy mixture that was. In personal matters, Cheetah was always a sweetheart but when he went out, he would get completely off the hook and cause all kinds of trouble, I stopped letting him borrow my clothes after a while because he would come home to my place after a night of debauchery with my fine threads all chewed up and destroyed. Anyway, the rotating line-up of Shotgun

Rationale rotated its way into including both Cheetah from the Dead Boys and Bob from the Replacements. You can only imagine the mayhem. I remember way before Cheetah arrived in Minneapolis, Bobby was constantly calling me about "shop" questions.

Bob asked, "Oh, what kind of guitar will he bring? Oh, what gauge strings does he use? Oh, what kind of plectrums does he use?"

Finally, Cheetah arrived in Minnesota at the rehearsal studio where he stood in front of Bob for the first time. I said, "Bobby Stinson, here is Cheetah Chrome." The first thing Bobby said to Cheetah was "Bend over!" Cheetah really liked that kind of humor and they got along famously. At shows, they would reach over each other's guitars and then play on each other's guitars. What I mean is that they would reach over and would be fingering the chords on the other's guitar while kissing each other on the lips. No lie! Very funny stuff and quite a sight to behold.

There isn't much mentioned in the various writings on the Minnesota music scene about the collaboration between Bob and I. Bob always attributed this to the fact that I was from New York and thus designated as an outsider. To me, this is simply another case of journalists trying to re-write history to suit themselves somehow. I guess they are probably boxed inside their own heads and want to write their own version of things. Also, at the time, I didn't wear those plaid shirts that everyone and their mother's uncle were wearing in Seattle and Minnesota (Hee! Hee! Now the bands in Minnesota dress like I do!).

Bobby and I were really close "brothers" and he opened his heart to me. I knew for sure how much he loved music because he always expressed that. He once asked me "Sonny would you die for music?" I didn't know exactly what he meant but from my point of view I said "No." Bob then looked at me with a deep, soulful, yet sarcastic look and said "Yeah, well I would." And in some universe where that would be required, I knew that Bobby would have died for music. Bob's playing had and will always have a profound effect on music fans and musicians. Whenever and wherever there are young musicians who are looking for real role models of the true rock 'n' roll feeling and spirit...Bobby will be right there for them to discover and to be inspired by.

The last time I saw Bobby was in a club in Minneapolis called First Avenue. I was on tour as Moe Tucker's (Velvet Underground) guitarist and I put Bobby on the guest list. A few months before that I had been on tour with Bobby in Europe with one of our Shotgun Rationale line-ups. The last show of our European tour was in a place called Enger, Germany. At this show, Bobby was singing with me, together on my microphone, which he knew from past shows was something I didn't prefer. The main reason is that sometimes the singing he was doing didn't have much to do with the song we were playing. Once in Chicago, I warned Bob to never do that again. And now here he was again, bellowing like crazy in Enger, Germany. Anyway, I swung at him and connected to his neck (later some audience members said they thought that was part of our act, fighting). After I slugged him Bob stayed away from my microphone. But after a few more songs Paul (Paul Smith - Guitar) came up to me and said, "Bobby's naked again!" I looked over to Bob's side of the stage just in time to see him running naked into the audience. Madness all around but a high-octane show, nevertheless.

Back to our last meeting at First Avenue. For some strange reason when we saw each other we ran to each other like a friggin Hallmark greeting card commercial. We embraced and I gave Bob a kiss on the side of his neck. Right on the same spot where I punched him in Germany. Then Bob said, "Hey, when is the next round in Europe?" He meant round as in boxing and round as in touring. The dry humor, always. Meaning he was ready for another tour even though the last one was grueling and crap for money. After that show at First Avenue with Moe and Sterling, I said goodbye to Bobby, I didn't know it, but it would be the last time I would see him. Sometimes I get the idea that there must be an angel up there somewhere that made sure that the last encounter I had with Bob was sweet. It's so strange that my kiss landed right where I had previously punched him onstage! Bob was really unique and special, I have tons and tons of sweet, funny, and wild stories about him, he was special and I'm sure all his fans and anyone who knew him as a friend always miss him. God bless you, Bobby.

# God's Chosen Drummers

*Memorial to Scott Asheton. Miss you always, Sonny*

I would like to share something in here somewhat personal, sad, mysterious, and somehow very important to me. Anyone who knows me knows that I am absolutely crazy about drummers. I swear, I have spent entire days, if not weeks, solely thinking about Charlie Watts and what a perfect creation he is. Sometimes I listen to Charlie so intensely the world disappears. The same goes for Jerry Nolan, Mitch Mitchell, Keith Moon, Machinegun Thompson, Rat Scabies, tons of Motown dudes, many, many drummers all the way to Luis from Bell Gardens, California. Sure, I do listen to all the parts in music but there is something about the drums that cannot be bullshitted. Lots of dudes can play a bunch of rehashed riffs on a guitar and polish em up but there is no polish that can create a groove and the kind of passion a drummer must provide. Maybe for some music, but not for my kind of rock 'n' roll. Sometimes when I listen to music, I blot out everything else and only listen to what's going on with the drums. Don't get the wrong idea, I can get by without food or human companionship simply by listening to the guitar on "I Want You Back" by the Jackson 5 or better yet something by the MC5! But there is always this extra attraction for me that the drums provide. The drums transport a lot of the passion in my world. That brings me to my pal Scott Asheton, the drummer of The Stooges. I first met him in Detroit back in the day and then later in the '80s when he and Rob Tyner were at a show of mine in Detroit. I hit it off with Scott right away and in no time, we were laughing and goofing off like bad delinquents. Later I invited Scott to play drums on a song for one of my albums (Roller Coaster). Again, at those sessions in NYC, we got along great and had tons of laughs. Later that year I asked Scott if he wanted to do a tour with me. The Stooges had long before broken up, as well as the Sonic Rendezvous Band. He occasionally did some shows with Scott Morgan and filled in with his brother and Niagara's band Dark Carnival sometimes, but generally, Scott was picking up manual labor whenever and wherever he could. I remember one time he told me he was digging fence pole holes at a farm in Michigan and this was in the winter. A fuckin' crime that a drummer so great and killer had to be regulated to shit work to feed his kids. Between him and his dedicated wife (she worked part-time as a nurse), they struggled through very tough times. Anyway, sometime during the '80s. I had asked Scott to do a U.S. tour with me, but he couldn't...for reasons, I don't wanna say here because it's his biz. We talked a lot on the phone though (I was living in Minneapolis back then and he was in the Detroit suburbs.) During one of the phone calls, he said he sent me something in the mail. A few days later I received a large pack of flyers that he had run off at a copy shop. He called again and said "Yeah, hey Sonny! I figured that since you were hitting nearly every town in the USA and Canada you could post these flyers around the clubs and the hip areas where you go and maybe I could get some work teaching drums, at least that's not gonna be outside in the ice-cold." I swear that's exactly what he said. Folks, can you fuckin' believe it? I put the flyers around and he didn't even get any calls! But that's not the saddest part. For me, it is simply a crime through and through. That the drummer of the fuckin Stooges, one of the monolithic greats is sitting at his kitchen table hand drawing a motherfucking flyer, to get work. After writing his name, he lists the albums he played on. Then he draws a lightning bolt on the middle of the page and his wife or kids color it in with crayons??? This is beyond fuckin' belief. But it's a true, cold fact. Could you imagine Ringo Starr having to do this?? Ummm... yeah...Ummm, let's see...Name –Ringo Starr Ummm... Experience ...Ummm yeah let's put it at the bottom...

Ummm Abbey Road, Meet the Beatles, Sgt. Pepper. ABSURD, no? This whole thing made me dizzy and a bit tearful at times. Later Scott was in my band, we recorded albums together, and did tours. I always told him if Iggy ever called, he could just ditch me in Kansas or wherever we were. And I have never parted from this flyer. Normally it is not more than 50 feet away from me. When I travel it's in my bag. It's part of me, like my skin, where I go that flyer goes. I reminded Scott of it years later when we were on tour in Europe. I showed it to him, and he laughed. We had many good times together and considering my fixation on great fucking drumming you can imagine it was heaven for me to work with him. A lot changed since Scott sent me that flyer. The Stooges reunited and both Scott and Ron were able to enjoy the glory they deserved after some long living in a sort of limbo/shadow. And also, the money came to Scott when he played huge festivals around the world with the reunited Stooges. No more digging fence post holes in the ground in the winter in Michigan. It all made me very happy for him. My brother.

*Since I wrote this story Scotty passed away. I'm so very glad he finally got to enjoy the recognition of adoring fans and colleagues as well as touring the world with Jim and his brother Ron. RIP Scotty, Love Sonny

# From Prayer Book:
# Praise to the Gods

*Bucky 23:18*

Say: Long live the space invading reptiles!

Down with everything except the ones we call "The Alien Right-wing People Eaters." Pray-nourish ARPE. I cut off my own head and offer it as food to the alien reptilian God. Praise to the underwater underdog of the deep. THE Evil God Shark Eye. For centuries he can see through the false Gods and bite them on the hindquarters. God Shark Eye God, why do the scholars and writers neglect you? Why did the Egyptians draw you on parchment and stone only to erase you later and draw over you and purposely cover up your existence?? A conspiracy well enacted by the Zionist Bowling Club. Even as you are the right hand of Satan you want to bite off that right hand. Don't you? My hungry cute little Shark God you are so romantic compared to other cranky Gods. Rise God Shark Eye and eat the Republicans and Democrats, I would tell you to eat the President too, but he tastes a little past his due date. Now as I call, rise God Shark Eye and eat all people. Glorify the reptilian race and become the first Shark to drive a brand-new Aquatic Volkswagen.

AMEN.

Love from the God trapped in a glass who will call you on your mobile telephone next week after I invade a small planet called "Earth Subdivision II."

AMEN.

# Church

"You get $100 a day and all the cocaine you can snort," read the ad on the laundromat's bulletin board. At first, I thought it was a joke, but you never know. The phone number to call was 666-1313. Was this just a prank or was the phone number another one of those strange unexplainable things that occur randomly in one's lifetime? I blew it all off as a joke. The next week I was at the same laundromat again. The sign I had seen the previous week was gone but in its place was another. It was written on the same type of stationary, which had a scene in the lower left-hand corner depicting two porpoises or dolphins frolicking in the surf. This time it read "Call 666-1212 for information about employment and spiritual advancement." Well, this was getting weird. I sat down on the laundromat bench and thought this whole thing over. I was staring down at the bench where various laundromat customers had carved their names and a variety of messages. There was "Chico Loves Sandra." There was "Born to Lose." There was "Led Zeppelin." There was also "For a good blow job call Carla." I wondered how many laundromats across America would have these same things written on the walls or carved into surfaces. But regardless of all the distractions and points of interest in the laundromat I couldn't stop looking at the sign on the bulletin board. I looked at it so many times that I began to think that if things could wear out from looking at them, this sign would now be nearly invisible. Then I thought if that were really true, Susan Klein would have no head because she sat in from of me in the 5th grade and I couldn't help but stare at her head all day long. Wow, what a cool idea! It would mean a thing would just disappear if it got looked at for too long or too many times. I thought hard about what the world would be like if this were true. The most beautiful girls would be only faintly there. Certain books in the library would be blank. And Elvis would have gone invisible by around his second album. All the time I was thinking these things, I was staring at the sign on the bulletin board. I suddenly got the feeling that everything that happened and every thought I had was being inspired by the laundromat. I felt stronger and more intelligent. To test my theory, I recited in Japanese the entire works of William Shakespeare. I was feeling so intelligent after this test I could barely stand it. I began leaping around the laundromat like a complete nutcase. But was this real? Was I smarter or was it just the whirring sound of the washers mesmerizing me? I decided to try another test. I took off the watch I had on my wrist. It was on old-fashioned watch with the hour, minute, and second hands. I was given this watch by an albino man in NYC. He said he was Haile Selassie but that he got caught in some kind of karmic time warp that changed his appearance. He was drunk and in pretty sad shape when I ran into him. He wouldn't stop bothering me unless I accepted his watch. He said he had waiting all his life to meet another traveler and I was to accept this watch as protection against karmic time warps. Anyway, I guess I was a traveler of some sorts. After all, I had in this year alone been to New Jersey, Cleveland, and Milwaukee. So, I accepted the gift from him and went on my way. Oh yes, back to the laundromat. So, as another test of my new abilities, I took the watch off and stomped on it with my boot. It broke into many pieces but at this point I forgot that I was going to do it as a test. I then became very dizzy and had to run into the bathroom to puke. Even puking was different. You see, usually when I puke. Oh, let's just skip that. Anyway, when I was done in the bathroom, I looked at the broken watch. I knew what I had to do. I collected all the parts, all the springs, sprockets, screws etc., and in 25 minutes with only the help of a toothpick, a grain of sand, a plastic liter bottle of Pepsi and just stuff from in the garbage can and around the laundromat, I fixed the watch. It was restored to complete working order. It looked a lot different. It was nearly twice the size it had been before, but it looked very interesting and it worked. I was looking at the bulletin board every 48 and 2/10ths of a second (my new version of my watch was actually improved over the old version as now it could clearly measure seconds in tenths of a second). I just couldn't stop looking at the sign on the bulletin board. Suddenly I passed out and came to 15 minutes and three tenths of a second later. In my unconscious dream sleep, I dreamed of dinosaurs living in the walls of my house. These dinosaurs were from planet Krazon. Oh! But pardon me! I don't have time to go into that here. Well I came to and stood up, a revelation. Oh, this laundromat, this beautiful magical laundromat. I loved this laundromat more than any man had ever loved any woman. I loved this sweet laundromat more than the greediest banker in the world loved money. This all-time greatest laundromat was all I could ask for. All a man could want. I stood there and suddenly all my madnesses stopped in unison. I knew what had to be done. Surely enough, I walked out of the door of the laundromat and three beautiful laundromat customers with lovely childlike eyes and friendly smiles were walking in. I knew what I had to do. I knew it in my mind. I knew it in my heart. It was my destiny and at this moment I realized that in my soul I knew it all along. I came back late that night when the laundromat was closed. It was actually 1:30 and 5 tenths of a second in the morning. It was so dark that if you closed your eyes it was lighter. I came well equipped. I brought a flashlight, a can of sardines, a sledgehammer, a butter knife, and a vintage $1,000 boombox with cassette and cd player. I broke into the laundromat through the front door. It was quite simple I just bashed off the fuckin' lock area with my robust new multi-function watch and the door opened, saving the sledgehammer for other activities. Boy, what a night. My muscles are still sore. After I got in, I basically smashed everything. First, by popping all the little round glass windows out of the washers and dryers with my sledgehammer. Then I caved in all the metal in the place. It was great fun. When I was done, I looked at my work. Ah, the sheer beauty. I felt more accomplished as an artist in that moment than at any other time in my life. The lines in the crumpled metal spoke of the metaphysical conflict between man's spiritual self and man's innate program of instincts. The broken glass on the floor and the random way it scattered, captured and reflected light with a mythopoetic sarcasm which was the sneer on the face of the Byzantine God that I carved onto the front door with the butter knife. All this, not to mention the calculated yet correct use of negative space in between the washers and dryers. All this was my greatest work to date. But the final brush stroke nearly killed me. My heart pounded so hard. My chest was heaving. The last element of my "active duty" artwork was so stunningly significant that I was nearly passing out installing it. I was blinded by my own sheer brilliance. In fact, a fission had occurred at this moment, separating myself from my brilliance. I was trembling and racing with adrenalin as I witnessed my own brilliance from an objective focal point. On top of the soap dispenser was an electrical wall- plug outlet. Here is where I installed the cassette/cd player. The CD player was loaded with a CD of Mozart's Requiem #3 and the cassette player was loaded with a special tape that was an 11-minute loop. I had earlier electronically adjusted everything, so the tape loop and the Requiem could be playing simultaneously. I set the player on top of the soap machine and plugged it in. It came on very loudly and synchronized in perfection. The tape loop was a recording of a woman giving birth. I turned the music up even louder and equalized the sound to suit the room. It was the most beautiful place in the world at that moment. I then set my flashlight up, so it pointed at the little sign on the bulletin board, spotlighting the notice about spiritual advancement. I never did call the number. The card alone was inspiring enough for me. God only knows what would happen if I actually called that number. My guess is that I would just vaporize. The inspiration in calling the phone number would be so intense that I would just become a transformative energy source in the form of vaporized matter and I only would be perceived on the cellular and soul level. But anyway, I didn't call. I became the first to view this energizing art installation. I only wished that every human being on earth could see it too. God, it was breathtaking. It was beyond perfection. Yes, if I must say it, I must. It was Holy. The laundromat had become a Holy sanctuary. A place where one could be and operate on the soul level. I began crying and I fell to my knees. I rolled to the ground in a fetal position and began to pull at my hair and clothes. All the sorrows and despondencies of life were now in my heart. I was crying so very much and there was much moaning, I could feel the power in my soul getting stronger. Suddenly, all at once I saw bright and brilliant light. Burning, crisp, exalted white light, filling every cell and molecule in existence. Then, all of a sudden, right in the middle of this holy cathartic experience, a car drove by and sounded its horn. The sound of the horn sounded as if it were a million miles away. It sounded like a sound that was made a million lifetimes ago. It had just reached me now. It was a familiar sound, and I knew it was profoundly significant, but I didn't know how. I ran outside and I could see the two red taillights of the car. They were going away. Traveling further and further away every second. I let it go. Although I knew there was a supremely holy significance to this car with its horn and lights. I could only speculate as it was totally gone now. But as I stood outside, it began to rain. Just kind of a drizzle. That faint whispery kind of drizzling. That sweet-muted love. An Eiffel-tower kind of light rain. With the rain there was a light. That soft blue smoke that passes light puffs mingling with the clouds and the muted light in a dimly lit after-hours night club. I realized then that I should get naked, for this could only be a true baptism. And Lord knows I did it. Oh, the sheer ease and serenity to it. I gently removed all my clothes and footwear. I stood there naked. in the drizzling rain, crying, "Oh God, thank you. Thank you for this experience." I could feel the coolness of the rain on my skin. I wanted for nothing. Everything was holy and perfect I was no longer the suffering, tortured man I once was. I was no longer the broken-hearted wretch of a loser as I had been before. I was an artist. A true living artist. An artist who had communed with God through his work. An artist whose life and work had suddenly fused into one expression. An artist, who through his art, had found total happiness. Oh, why was I chosen for this? Would they view, as I did, the laundromat as a city of holiness? Oh, how the world needed this vision. Oh, how I craved it for them. But was mankind finally done with its greed and striving? I prayed so. And now, now at that glorious moment I could see a sign. Humans were near. Oh, how beautiful they were. My mind was racing. My blood was pumping and flushing through my soul. Would they? Would they receive the gift? They drove up. It was a fine police car. Two fine and beautiful policemen came out of the car and walked up to me. I looked at them. My eyes filled with love, nobility, and benevolence. I said to them "Bless you, my brothers, you are the first." With a Bronx accent they said, "The first what?" And of course, I said "Please believe and trust me my brothers. You must now remove your clothes, for this is holy ground you are standing on. Come with me into the laundromat and be enlightened." What happened after this point is all a bit hazy to me. My recollection process is very weak at the moment. My memory is acting very chaotically and thought encapsulants are very jagged and come in a non-ordered sporadic barrage of mixed and distorted events. I now believe I must have vaporized at that point. I have just realized this during my writing of these last few sentences. So, I believe that although in a physical sense I'm at the moment writing these words, it's only a sort of physical reprieve. I have been given a final act to accomplish in the physical world and that is obviously the act of writing down these words for your enlightenment. At the moment, I'm only aware of the paper and the pen with which I write. I am totally and completely oblivious to my surroundings and, anyway, my focus is on you, dear and loving reader. I reckon, what I'm trying to say is this, to you:

You are now reading something that has been written by a man who was vaporized. I was vaporized and then later brought back to life to write this for you to read and learn from. I can feel the taste of light in my soul at this moment and I sense the re-vaporizing process is under way, so my time is short and haven't much more time for this writing. I will just say this. Love one another and do not be afraid to turn everyday objects and/or places into art projects. Do not judge one another, for the man you see eating food from a garbage can could actually be a performance artist or simply a hungry man. Hold each other near to your hearts for your time on earth is truly limited. And lastly, a warning: I don't know what it means or how it got there, I must have done it myself because it's my own handwriting. Moments ago, I looked at my forearm and I apparently scratched words into my skin with some glass. It's very clearly written and easy to read. It really does look like it must have been painful to write it and I'm convinced it's important. I guess I have to leave it up to you to figure it out because in a moment I will be once again be vaporized. Anyway, here it is, scratched into my skin, it says:

"Don't trust the police. They're dumb fucks."

I must go now.

Eternal love.

# Reform School Alumni

I grew up in Westchester County, New York. It was one of those idyllic suburbs but me and my friends were not really impressed. Anyway, I came from the bad side of town. I was part of a group of kids that were intent on destroying everything and anything that tried to force or train us to conform. We did considerable damage to the school in terms of the building and grounds as well as doing our best to disrupt classes. I think we were shocked at all the hypocrisy and lies around. I guess we were part of the youth revolution. At first, we ran around as little junior greasers. All Elvis, iridescent clothes, leather, black and white, sharp-dressing, and whatnot. My first favorite images were Eddy Cochran, Gene Vincent, the typical Wild Bunch type. But that was a bit for the previous generation and suddenly there were the Beatles, Stones, and Yardbirds. We were still pretty young but old enough to get into the music. That was the first really exciting rush that was ours. The music. Soon the hair got a little bit longer. I think when all the stuff like the Kinks and Yardbirds hit we were around 12 years old. But that was all we could get from the radio and older kids who had records. Soon I wanted to venture out to find stuff on my own. I made forays into Manhattan and saw bands like The Fugs and the whole Village scene. I was tall for my age and looked older than 13 so there were no problems for me navigating myself around the city. Also, even though I hated school I was a voracious reader and could relate to subjects that were usually more interesting to people older than myself.

The Village was going through the transition from the Beats to the Hippies. One weekend I was walking around the streets and the whole scene was very intense for a kid. I saw Bob Dylan on the street and accidentally wound up in the Factory at age 13 where Andy Warhol was showing a film. Quite impressive at that age, well any age I suppose!

In school, I was already in trouble most of the time. Mainly because of boredom and my hatred of authority. Detention was part of my curriculum. Later I wrote a song in Testors called Detention. Anyway, I quit school left home and hit the road at age 13½. After that, I had various incarcerations and did my share of jail time. First, it was a reform school in upstate N.Y. Usually, when I came into contact with the police, they would find substances in my pockets. Since they weren't allowed to actually kill me (as they would have enjoyed since they hated anything that looked like freedom) they had to take the second choice and incarcerate me. My first contact with the police was when I was a minor. They had to put me in reform school rather than give me hard jail time or execution, cock suckers!

Mostly like I said, I had difficulties adjusting to society. I didn't like having to conform to a corrupt authority, so for me, it was trouble from the start. Punk was a natural progression, I suppose. At age 11, I was already writing poems that were filled with semi-violent imagery that I later used in Testors songs, "I wanna blow holes in the sky and rip it up in pieces." (from the song "Primitive" by Testors) is an example.

At first, we didn't even have the term "punk." Me and Gene formed Testors in 1975 in New York City and the term punk and punk rock were not much in use at that time. So, I had no idea what to call our music when we started. When pressed to describe ourselves we called our stuff "Original Music." And added "you probably wouldn't like it." The closest term we knew of was hard rock. I imagined that meant even harder than rock and although we believed our rock was harder than the normal rock bands that were out at the time, we didn't really fit that category. In fact, a lot of the hard rock bands didn't even seem so hard to me! So, we called it "Original Music" until Legs and John came out with a magazine called *Punk*. From then on, the bands he wrote about were termed punk.

Anyway, punk isn't something you "get into." It's not something you choose. It's something you are. Like a progression, not something you choose like "Hmmm being a loving fuckin hippie is not giving me many benefits, think I'll try being a punk, maybe I can get some chicks that way!!"

No, it didn't work that way. To be honest, though none of us in the early New York scene liked the term punk at first, we began to own it after the words "New Wave" were foisted upon the scene. I thought, "What the hell is new wave? Watered down punk?"

It sounded really awful and made me want to puke.

After that new wave bullshit, punk felt o.k. It sounded tough and cool. New wave was some industry term to soften the image for the general public.

The beginnings.

Yeah, I was somewhere in my twenties and I leave NYC and travel down to Florida bringing my songs, a tape recorder, and my guitar with me. At that time around 1974, New York was pretty dead in terms of venues to play "Original Music," so I got frustrated and split. I wrote a bunch of songs there in Florida. While there, I met Gene and taught him my songs. One day I noticed a *Rock Scene* magazine at a 7-11 in Clearwater, Florida. I opened it up and was shocked. Suddenly, it looked like there was someplace in NYC to play and two groups, one called Television and the other called the Ramones, were already doing it! I'd like to personally thank the guys in Television for discovering and building the first makeshift stage in C.B.G.B.'s.

After reading that *Rock Scene* magazine, I grabbed Gene and my guitar, and we hightailed it to New York. I spoke to Willy DeVille (RIP) years ago and he told me he had a similar experience only he was in San Francisco (or maybe he said Connecticut). He also hightailed it back to New York after hearing that Television, Patti Smith, and the Ramones had cut through the jungle and found a place to play.

So, by the time I got back to NYC, there was a little scene forming and I was happy to finally have a place to play the music I had already written in a sort of void or vacuum. There were incredible moments at CB's and Max's, like seeing the Ramones for the first time and playing with the Cramps. Other musicians also inspired me during this time. I remember seeing Johnny Thunders playing and he was making the most authentic great sound with only his guitar and his amp. No pedals and no special effects. That was an inspiration, and I threw away my Echoplex the next day. I would much rather hear Johnny play his Gibson through an amp then hear the guy from Pink Floyd running a hundred effects.

Basically, the most inspiring aspect was the direct simplicity. Everyone was disinterested in the excess and rock star posing of the big groups that were popular at the time. There was a shift away from that stadium crap. All the music the current rock stars were playing was dead boring to us. There was a new fascination and obsession with the simplicity of the music from the '50s. So, there was a kind of divorce from the rich rock star music and a reconnection with the passion of real rock 'n' roll from the '50s and early '60s.

As for Testors, I already had a set of songs from my pre-Florida time, in addition to the songs I wrote down there. When I arrived back in NYC with Gene I wrote more and more, and we named the band and looked for other musicians to join us. Our music was very individualistic. I sort of worked in my own bubble, like a cave. I liked it quite raw, Gene and me were very connected in our guitar playing, since I taught him how to play.

New York in the '70s was pretty fuckin cool. There was no pattern to go by and we were writing the script as we went along. There were so many bands with original music. Music that was completely different from what was on the radio.

At first, there were no cool clothes around. If you

weren't lucky enough to have an older brother who you could steal 50's clothes from, you had to improvise. The music was the main thing of course, but I cannot emphasize enough how insanely passionate people were about their clothes. In C.B.G.B.'s, you would see guys with their bell-bottomed pants taped to make the bottoms look straight-legged. A style was forming but there was no stuff in the shops. I wondered "where the fuck did these people get those pointy shoes and straight pants??" I searched the fuckin city till I found em, but it was not easy in 1975, since all the shops still had the hippie stuff. It was cool because it was very narrow stylistically and it wasn't easy to get it right and when you saw other people who had it dialed in it was really inspiring. I still think some of them got those clothes from older brothers or uncles. It was a small group of people and there were intensely strict rules concerning what was cool and what was not. Like I said earlier, '50s stuff was cool. Homemade stuff was cool. Scary stuff was cool. Anything disgusting was cool. And they all worked on it all the time. I remember my managers at the time asking me to tone down my image because they felt the girls might view me as a serial killer or an escaped convict. Of course, now if someone dressed like that it wouldn't be so shocking. You can sit at a family dinner these days and be accepted.

"More stuffing with your turkey dinner, Billy?"

But back then, certain looks really shocked the hell out of people. It could be very scandalous to show up at a certain function dressed Zooed Out. And it also was strange for us to suddenly realize that the image was even more powerful than we thought possible. People would scream insults at us when we walked down the streets!

C.B.G.B.'s and Max's Kansas City were the main places. At first, they were the only places for me to hang out. Later there were a few more cool places. They were sort of geared for the party scene and not the music.

C.B.G.B.'s had that street vibe, and it was really was focused on the music. Of course, there was a lot of drinking and debauchery, but the main issue and focus was the music and the bands. Later you can see a lot of situations/places where it became the opposite. Where the party was the main thing and the music secondary (I noticed that at the Limelight later). A fuckin disco that featured live music as well.

Max's was always glorious. I remember that Max's had a curtain. The black curtain was closed across the stage and then you were announced. Whoosh! The curtain was opened. Very exciting and mysterious with that curtain. Max's definitely had the uptown art vibe. I think the Velvet Underground played the first-ever show there. Then later it was the glitter bands. Later, it was full-on punk. C.B.G.B.'s and Max's were so important in allowing a stage for the new bands to play. Sometimes real Rock Stars would show up and they often looked very out of place. Imagine it. You have a very grassroots scene going on in C.B.G.B.'s and suddenly a rock star shows up and strides in with a couple of bodyguards. It just didn't seem to be cool in any way to show up with bodyguards, perhaps smart and prudent, but definitely out of place.

It must have looked like a perverse kindergarten to those guys.

The best shows I played with Testors were certainly those in the beginning at C.B.G.B.'s and Max's. At first, we played shows without a bass player. We tried out all the possible candidates in NYC to be our bass player, but we couldn't find someone suitable, so we decided to go for it without a bass player. Two guitars and drums. I remember the guy at Max's saying, "Hey, where is youse-guyzez-bassplay-yah?"? I said, "We don't use one." And the guy was actually pissed off, like as if we had ripped him off or cheated him somehow.

At C.B.G.B.'s, it was never questioned. We just turned our guitars louder and didn't give a fuck. Later we added a bass player because he was a pal who wanted to play. But those first years as a three-piece were quite unique. Later we had a different drummer and a bassman. That was very cool too because then we could do other kinds of songs and approaches.

Our worst gig wasn't so bad because it was charged and exciting. But it wasn't in New York. It was at the Hot Club in Philly. The bands from C.B.G.B.'s and Max's discovered it. I think Stiv told me about it. Well, it was only a two or three-hour drive and it was a cool place to play our stuff. When Testors played there our first time there was a band opening for us that was a sort of standard rock band. They had a number of fans in the club that night. They played their set for their friends and fans. I remember they kind of sounded like the stuff you would hear on the radio. I don't think their audience was ready for Testors. We were in our early format that was three-piece with mainly fast, raw, brutal songs. Someone announced us:

"From New York City! TESTORS!"

We slashed into our songs. After a couple of songs, the crowd was yelling things like "Learn how to play!!" and "Go back to New York." Really! They were shocked and even insulted. So, I told them to inform their mothers that I would be coming over to their houses after our show for some sex and a nice warm meal. Then they went berserk. They pulled Gene off the stage and the P.A. speakers came tumbling down to the ground. There were also some fans of ours in the audience so the whole place turned into a sort of punch out. We continued to play but we only made it through three more songs and then the whole thing was shut down by the cops. It was a mess. When we were done, there was broken glass everywhere, plus broken wood from chairs. Someone flooded the bathrooms so there was a lake of water as well. Complete mayhem! You have to try to realize these fuckers and their view of us. We were wearing clothes that were totally strange to them.

77

They were actually very angry about our clothes and that got them all nervous and excited, then when we played our raw music, they could not stand it anymore, and they went mental!! This was pretty early and before all the hardcore bands came out in the '80s. The people in Philly never heard stuff so fast and raw. They figured it must be crap. They thought it sucked and they were screaming! They really had a huge negative reaction!

The next time we played there was a year later and by then a lot of people in Philly were into the music and we didn't have to play to people who were against us!! Also, I was writing some more melodic songs (a bit more), we still played our slash and burn stuff (which is still my favorite stuff from then, the angst-ridden downstroke songs) but we had a few darker deeper structures going on as well by then.

Ron was the guy who for a short time became our first bass player. He called himself "Rex Pharaoh." He was a surrealist painter and one of his early works, a painting he did in 1974, was titled *Kill Me*. As I remember it the painting had a skull guy with a snake going through the eye socket and it had a text below saying "Kill Me." Later we were making T-shirts and I made one that looked like someone puked on it. It was with this stuff called "Puff Paint." Then Ron made a black T-Shirt with large white letters on it saying "Kill Me." He was all over the city in that T-Shirt and later a book had a similar title. I understand that Richard Hell had a similar T-Shirt and later Richard Lloyd began to wear it. I'm not sure if they saw Ron traversing the city in his shirt or if it was a crazy coincidence. I do know Ron made the painting in Florida around 1974.

But as I know it that was Ron's image and he paid dearly for it. Eventually, a guy in the subway knifed him really bad and Ron had to go to the hospital for a long time. He survived but was very shaken. He quit the band and left NYC after that.

The city was very rough. Gangs roaming. Junkies

everywhere. 42nd street was worse than the movies portray. I used to walk down 42nd street between 6th and 7th Ave late at night and challenge myself to not give way to anyone on the sidewalk. Nobody was with me, so it wasn't a matter of impressing someone. I just was sick of the jungle and the whole pecking order in Manhattan at the time. A real fuckin zoo. I walked down that street at 1 in the morning in a straight line. There were pimps dressed in lime green fuzzy clothes and huge brim hats, obviously alternating between holding their gun under their belts to holding their dicks. Usually alongside them parked on the street was some huge Cadillac with a metal flake paint job. There were pimps, thieves, and lowlifes every inch on the sidewalk. Hustling and talking loudly. But I didn't budge. If the other one didn't move there would be a collision. I refused to give way, just walked right at them. Begrudgingly they moved, probably figuring it was better to move than to have a street conflict over nothing. It was a sort of confidence builder for me. Although in another way it was a suicide mission, almost a death wish. But the way I grew up and the dynamic in my childhood made me feel the need to find out who I was in NYC. I already knew who I was in my childhood home, I was the one who was abused and tortured. If I let the people who raised me choose my place in life, I would have been the lowest dog, anywhere. So, I walked down that street and didn't move for anyone… I'd have rather died than move. Sorry that that might sound dramatic or tough. But it is true.

I could really spend some time describing NYC and what it was like at the time. The city was in default. The middle class had moved out. Graffiti everywhere, garbage, death, and violent drug deals on the street. You name it. But it was ours. There was a flourishing music and art scene and cheap rents. Not some playground for NYU students like it is now.

There were lots of troubled people around the scene.

When I first began hanging around C.B.G.B.'s I called a lot of the delinquents in Westchester and said, "You really have to come down here, there are tons of fuckers just like us." But they never came, they either went to jail or were stuck in their lives. Often time stuck in the music they knew as teenagers and not able to bridge the gap between Hendrix and Patti Smith or the Beatles and The Dead Boys. For me, that was a logical progression. In terms of off the hook behavior and mentally ill actions, I saw a lot. I remember once I was at the bar at CB's and there were only around 10 people in there. Some guy took a photo of Legs and suddenly Legs screamed out "No photographs!" Then he grabbed the camera and struggled to the ground with the guy in a real wrestling match. We all sat there amazed thinking that in reality Legs would be wishing that someone took his photo. Not too mentally ill, but amusing. The mental stuff came in the form of various dramas and destructive behavior. I really don't want to gossip and tell stories about people who might feel the story is not so flattering. And although some people had some deep psychological challenges these same people could also be very sweet. I really loved Dee Dee and we had a nice rapport and easy-going alliance. But Dee Dee could really go off the hook and ruin everything. Smashing stuff and insulting people. I would say that generally most of the people in the scene had issues of some kind that stemmed from a destroyed or compromised childhood experience. Let's put it this way. The fuckin public and the radio had The Eagles and we had C.B.G.B.'s, Max's, and The Ramones. The one side had songs about a "Peaceful Easy Feelin." The other had songs about sniffin' glue. Yes, it's true it was a real charged and dysfunctional mess, but it was also a scene teeming with people who needed to express a lot of things. Not the least of these expressions were anger and discontent.

Most of the people I knew in NYC had already taken every kind of drug available and known to exist at the time. Many of them had left behind the psychedelic drugs though. At C.B.G.B.'s in the beginning, we always played two sets, an early set and a late one. Usually, only two or three bands playing on a given night. Because we were new bands at the time none of us had enough songs for two completely different shows so we would just repeat the same songs in the second set. One night we played with the Cramps and I remember between sets they told me they were going to take some LSD in order to watch Testors play and then do their second set. This was incredible to me because it had been a long time since I met anyone who was taking LSD. It was beyond comprehension that they would play a show on it! Recently our original drummer told me he took it for playing shows sometimes. Amazing! But in general, the hippie drugs were not the style on the NYC punk scene. A lot of people experimented with heroin and a lot of them made it a lifestyle. I did it for a short while and discovered I liked it too much. I have a strong will and when I saw the direction, I was going in I quit. I can say that Testors was not at all a band frequently involved in drugs. We were virtually "straight edge" except for a few bumps in the road and did drugs only occasionally. We were very rigid with ourselves in terms of how we played the music, and I don't believe we could have done it the way we wanted if we were all downed out.

I don't have anything against people using drugs. It's their right and it's their choice. I have seen Johnny Thunders play sets more energetic and passionate while fully whacked on heroin than other people who were straight as a judge. So, it can go. But then again on a certain night, Johnny was too messed up to play well. I think heroin had a mixed effect on the NYC scene. It did wreck some of the momentum of the artists and their output. The drug does have an alluring "pull" to say the least. It's like a lover who is nothing but trouble! Who the fuck wants to run around with sores on their hands and unhygienic crap all around? Not me! I was more into the music and showed the pain and angst in the songs.

Also, I believe that a lot of people who come from a disturbed or dysfunctional background are often involved in a process of self-medicating. Heroin is one of those drugs. You don't usually see a person on heroin jumping up at a disco flaunting themselves around. They are usually alone and dealing in a way with some inner pain. Surely some people will jump on a bandwagon and think it's a fashion and I always pitied those types. Strange how being destroyed inside and shooting dope, to deal with the pain, can also be appropriated as fashion by some people. In the end, though the dope is all a waste of time, because there is nothing transformative. Things usually get worse. It is a sort of giving up. And this is the reverse of the original attitude in NYC. Some of the attitude and bravado came from drugs but I believe the actual attitude expressed in the music at the time came mostly from a deeper dissatisfaction with the status quo and the whole set up of our society. Seeing the hypocrisy and lies all around was the main motivator for people I knew. We had the feeling we could change the world. I am serious about that.

For us, it was something incredible and dreamlike. We had only been playing C.B.G.B.'s, Max's, and the Hot Club in Philly, very small nightclubs. The show we did there in the CBGB 2nd Ave theater was with the original line-up of Testors, Me, Gene, and Gregory. Two guitars and drums. It was quite early on. It was our understanding that they were handpicking bands from C.B.G.B.'s to play the theater. We couldn't believe it that we could play the theater. Part of the setup and scene there was that the show was played live over WPLJ and after the show, the band was interviewed live on the radio. Everything was played live on the radio as well as being recorded. We were thinking only Blondie and Patti could play there. But we were chosen. And we were on cloud 9, lemme tell you. I would give a lot to have that tape from our performance that day, I know it exists somewhere. We were in top form and it was probably our best show till that point. It was all so exciting for us! We even had to buy longer guitar cables because the stage was so much larger than the ones we knew. A real old theater with seats and a balcony. So very impressive and exhilarating for us! I remember looking at the huge velvet curtain and huge wooden stage floor and saying to Gene, "Wow! Man! Just like Hendrix!"

Anyway, it all was going along fine. We played but when it came time to be interviewed Richard Hell and Lenny Kaye showed up and were in the process of taking up all our interview time. I sat in the audience for a while listening as Richard and Lenny were discussing the virtues of Rimbaud and then got up in utter disgust, left the theater, and went across the street to a record store. At the record store were people who had just watched us play and they were having a little party. I drank quite a lot of Jack Daniels with them and for the first time in my life, I snorted a shit load of cocaine. Then I looked at the clock grabbed the hand of a pretty girl and went back to the theater. We sat with Gene and Gregory while Richard and Lenny were still off to the French Existentialist races. I asked the technician, "How much time is left for the interview part here?" He said, "Around 8 minutes." I tried to talk Gene and Gregory into crashing the podium but they wouldn't. After all, it was a theater, and it was dark, and the podium was lit. I can understand they were intimidated. But I really didn't care so I went up myself and the whole thing turned into chaos, with me falling around the podium, smashing things, very drunk and fucked up, and them (Lenny, Richard, and the Moderator) looking very surprised. I pulled Lenny's chair out from under him and a fight ensued. The mics were ripped out and eventually, the entire thing was shut down. This was the first part of Testors being 86'ed temporarily from C.B.G.B.'s. Later I became friends with Lenny and Richard played bass on a song on my album Roller Coaster. We all got past the event. And that was my Second Avenue C.B.G.B.'s Theater experience. But where is that tape? I did manage to grab ahold of one of the live microphones during the scuffle and yelled some obnoxious stuff across the airwaves!

Truth is we were playing shows and doing our music in NYC since late 1975, early '76. True, we never recorded with Sire or made an album. True, I never was in bed with Seymore, bla, bla, bla. And we shied away from record company assholes. So, we did not have an album out back then which meant that people who didn't see us live wouldn't hear us know us and our music. I hated the term new wave when it came out and also power pop but I can understand if people only heard the single that's how they would view us. Fact is we were some kind of underdogs on the early scene. We played faster and louder than most of them and the only bands that took us under their wings were the Cramps and The Dead Boys. Nobody else would dare play a show with us because we were ferocious and tight. But anyone in CB's during the 1975-1978 era who saw us were witnessing the only band from those days who could seriously be considered as a pre-hardcore ancestor. Just put on any early Testors song like Primitive, I See, Madras Prison, Don't Tell Me, Remembrance. Fast, brutal, and usually only two parts in the songs that lack any sort of melody. When the hardcore scene developed, I was very fuckin pleased!

We had been playing shows at Max's since late 1975, Tommy Dean booked our first date. And after that, we had our first show at C.B.G.B.'s. Just getting those first shows was a monumental task since everyone was already sucking each other's dicks and there was not much left for us in terms of space to play. At the beginning of 1975 we rehearsed a lot on 7th Ave and 21st street, we were rehearsing with full enthusiasm and by the time we played, we were burning with passion and energy. Finally, we got booked at Max's, we played only on Monday,

Tuesday, and Wednesday nights at Max's and CB's. The ultimate shit nights for the ultimate underdogs. We played our hearts and souls out in those rooms. We did have a following and we did have an impact, but we were regulated to the off nights. Sometimes I meet people from bands from back in those days who never saw us! Some people mainly went out on weekends. But when I do run into people who saw us, they remember it well. I get some incredible feedback from them.

Once in a while, we had managers, but they always quit and ran for the hills when they came up against our no compromise attitude and protocol. I sometimes tried to please them. They would say things like, "Sonny your image and clothes make the women think you are some kind of escaped lunatic or a serial killer, don't you think you could tame it down?" Really, they asked me this!!! So, I wore some tight slacks and a dinner jacket and sure enough, my success with the ladies improved. But I really didn't care for that game and didn't like being manipulated to change. It did at that moment seem that people around me wanted something.

Then came the event. The "Time Is Mine"/"Together" conundrum. Like I said before, the early Testors stuff was quite primitive in structure. I had no interest in Rock Stardom or even basic commercial concerns so for me, the songs were perfect expressive vehicles. And the fact that they only had two parts was fine with me, why meander around. Just get to the point. But I did begin to wonder if I was able to write songs with a more traditional structure and melody line. After all, this is what was considered talented and professional by many around. So, one day I sat in the Bronx with my guitar and wrote "Time Is Mine" and "Together." More or less as an experiment., I wrote them both in a day. For sure the lyrics were something I was feeling but I tried to write the music part in a more pop way. Well, I brought those two songs to the rehearsal room and played them for the guys as a sort of lark. "Hey, check out what I did." But instead of just checking them out and saying "cool," they wanted to learn them and seemed pretty much excited by the two songs.

Fast forward a few weeks later to Bleeker Bob. The wisest wise ass guy in all of punkdom. Bob offered to be our manager. This meant we would have to withstand Bob's verbal abuse and jibes more often than if we only met him when we frightfully looked into his record shop, mistakenly thinking he was not there, only to enter, and be shocked to see he was there! Deep down inside this guy was the prototypical warm-giving New York Jew with a heart of gold. But on the outside, he could be very crude and abrasive. This was our manager, "Oh look the cocksuckers from Testors just walked in!!" Not exactly Brian Epstein. One evening we went to his shop for our weekly abuse and he wanted a contract. He said, "Only you Sonny, the other assholes can wait outside." So, the guys left the shop and waited outside on the street in front of the glass window. In the backroom, Bob scrawled some stuff on a piece of yellow legal paper and said, "Sign it or fuck off!" I read it and I'm pretty good at contract reading. Most of the ones I have signed have said, "You are being screwed" between the lines. This one was no different. I brought it out to the guys and said: "Guys, if we sign this, we will never see a penny for our efforts, if we don't sign it, we don't get a single out." We put the yellow sheet of paper on the record store window and signed it. Still, we have never seen a cent, but Bob did get the record out there. Next was the meeting with the band at Mollies' on 7th Ave and 31st Street. They wanted to do "Time Is Mine" and "Together" as the single. It was a band meeting. I wanted to record "I See" and "Primitive." My argument was that this was what Testors was all about. They knew those songs would never ever get within a hundred miles of a radio station in 1979 (we recorded it late 1979 and it got out in '80). Sure, they were right, and the truth is we had been slashing and burning all over the place but without much advancement. I know young men can be prone to wonder about their lives and their futures and I do believe this was at play. They wanted to record those two songs because they felt they had the most commercial possibilities. I wasn't interested in all that, but I gave up under pressure. I made a deal that we would record those two songs in the studio but right after that, we would record all our other stuff in our own loft on 4-track. When it came time to record the two, I pushed the energy as far as the songs would tolerate and tried to bring them the most feeling I could. But for me, the real glory came with recording the rest of my songs. I like the two songs and enjoy playing them, but they don't have the same level of desperateness the rest of the material has. One of the best moves in my life was to bargain to record the other songs directly.

Testors was very focused on keeping our music real and without any compromise. Eventually, we broke up mainly because it became nearly impossible to keep it going without any substantial support. Like I have said, a lot of that inability to fit in at the time was due to my strong desire to never compromise. We had offers but they always came with a request for us to make our music a bit more easy listening. "Slow down, play in a commercial way." They always wanted us to compromise and play slower and nicer. Sometimes I said, "Yeah thanks but, no thanks." But usually I just told 'em to fuck off!

Things were progressing for us in some ways. We did have fans and people who thought the music we were committed to was special. Our shows were very rewarding for us but without progress in terms of money and advancement, questions began to arise. Some of the guys started having those nagging career concerns that often are on the minds of people at that age. As I told you in the section about "Time Is Mine"/"Together," people in the band started to wonder if the no compromise way was the right way for them. They also began to consider things like University and a future. Or maybe a real job. It happens. Who can blame a guy? It's hard to struggle and strive for years, very hard. People begin to question their path and consider a future and family and security. I can't blame them. It's natural but this development and doubt was sneaking into our dream. For me, it was an easier decision because I had a clear vision, and I was the songwriter. Also, sometimes I am a bit of a romantic, so I thought it was valid to continue on the no compromise path. Even though I knew there was no possibility of getting on the radio. I didn't believe the songs "Time Is Mine" and "Together" would be on the radio anyway. After all, there was no promotion at all. It simply 'came out' which basically meant it was in Bob's store and a thousand of them made their way to Australia of all places! Add to that stuff the fact that the scene in NYC was getting soft until hardcore hit. Some of the bands were really kissing the record companies' asses by trying to be more commercial with that fuckin new wave. Also, it seemed like all over the scene people were more interested in which party they were invited to and it became different. Drugs and parties began to take first place over the "commitment to music and change" that existed before. I was still involved with feelings of changing the world or at least shakin' it up. The party scene was boring to me. Hanging around fucked up, just didn't do it for me. I liked to get fucked up sometimes, but the music was my focus. Also, I didn't care much about the future. I always felt that at any moment a car could smash you into bits and then it's over anyway. When I saw some of the resolve being compromised in Testors I decided to end the group while it was still vital and had meaning rather than let it fizzle out and become something different.

The scene was changed, bands were getting slower, bands were selling out. People (artists?) were arriving in NYC financed by Mommy and Daddy and they were buying out all the cheap apartments. The art scene was more or less filled with people who could afford a loft to the tune of three grand a month. Not much real art but lots of fake galleries and free glasses of champagne. And unfortunately, like I said earlier, some of the best bands were totally train wrecked on heroin. Shortly after Testors broke up I had a NYC band called The Primadonnas. Although the music was pretty good, the band was mostly a drug deal. Joey was selling Quaaludes to Luigi. Luigi was selling coke to Kenny. It was a joke. The drummer would drop his sticks at our rehearsals and that meant it was time to do cocaine. Sometimes I liked to get fucked up too, but the music was the main thing to me, nothing came before that. I really felt the integrity in the sound and playing was more important than the party scene New York was turning into.

So, I left NYC with a girl from Minnesota, and went from living in New York City on Bleecker across from CB's to living in Minneapolis, Minnesota. Now that was something that was very bizarre for me. Maybe 'bizarre' is a big word when talking about a geographical relocation, but a word that fits. Biz-fuckin-zare.

I turned on the TV on the first morning there were farm reports all over the screen! People driving really slowly on the highway, I was used to people driving faster on the West Side Highway which was only two lanes and these people were crawling down the interstate!!! They had a sort of slow-talking style as well. Just a lot different from NYC. The slums in Minnesota looked like nice Victorian wooden homes to me, compared to the burnt husks of buildings on the lower east side of Manhattan in the late '70s that I lived around. The slums in Minneapolis were actually really nice structures that simply needed some paint. And there I was in the center of this easy-going mid-west culture with a switchblade in my pocket!

On my first day there I had visited a shopping mall and then later I was walking around near the main park in town and people were pointing at me. Really looking and scratching their heads. It's hard to imagine now, but to them, I looked like some sort of alien or something. It was really weird. I had to tell someone back home, so I went to a telephone booth and called Johnny Thunders. The conversation went something like this.

Sonny: "I tell you it's weird out here, today I was walking through a shopping mall in my black pants and Beatle boots and the people were pointing at me saying, 'Devo! Devo!' What the fuck is that all about?"

Johnny: "Ahhhh, Sonny they never saw nuthin lookin' like you, the only group that got record distribution so far out there is Devo, so anything they haven't seen yet is 'Devo' to them. Haa! haaa!"

Sonny: "Yeah, but Devo wears garbage bags, astronaut suits, and flowerpots on their heads. I don't look like that."

Johnny: "To them you do. Haa! Haa!!"

After a while, I got a bit settled and bought a house and it took some time till I started venturing out. But finally, after a month or two I did start checking things out and the first group I saw was Hüsker Dü. I was really amazed. I went up to them and said they had the energy and spirit that was all around in NYC a few years before and I said that I missed that!! They took it as a compliment, and we became friends. Later I moved into a building that was all artists' lofts and Bob Mould was my next-door neighbor. He was really a good guy and lent me some equipment sometimes. And a few years after that Greg Norton was in my band Shotgun Rationale for a short while, we did a tour of Canada together. Minnesota was quite a culture shock for me at first but eventually, I came to love the place. Also, I had a long friendship and played with Bobby Stinson there.

I thought it was sad that while I was in Minnesota CBGB closed. It was the big business mentality once again. They wanted to close C.B.G.B.'s so they could enjoy the gentrification free for all. And I don't care what people say about Hilly. Last time I was there he was still humping cases of beer from one spot to another. He was one of the greatest supporters of American music and he doesn't get the credit he deserves. He wasn't only after money like the others who came later into that area with the gentrification fever. The guy was very soulful. He supported American music that went the distance from Patti Smith's poetry to the Hardcore Matinee days. Hilly is missed and the house he built is missed.

When I go to that area these days, I can have an 80-dollar meal and gaze at the taxis that go by. I really didn't have the foresight to imagine back in the times when we wallpapered those walls around there with our flyers that it would turn into what it has. Everything changes but the greedy fuckers never change. I signed the petition to insist that C.B.G.B.'s be designated as a historical site. It was the home of a certain stage of American music and I think some respect should have been shown for the artists and creativity that was born there. I suppose in France they would have preserved the place, but we know greed often wins in America. This is sad but true. NYC is still special- I still feel it has a special energy level. Maybe it's a special yuppie energy level, for now, I don't know. The apple is definitely more polished these days. I miss the feeling of chaos I felt on the street. But New York will always be a magnet and attract creative people. There is a magic there that anyone can feel, and I don't think it's possible for the greedy fuckers to ever steal that magic.

# Out Soon On Far West

farwestpress.com